HEARTLAND

ALSO BY WILSON HARRIS

Fiction:
Palace of the Peacock
Far Journey of Oudin
The Whole Armour
The Secret Ladder
The Eye of the Scarecrow
The Waiting Room
Tumatumari
Ascent to Omai
The Sleepers of Roraima
The Age of the Rainmakers
Black Marsden
Companions of the Day and Night
Da Silva da Silva's Cultivated Wilderness and Genesis of the Clowns
The Tree of the Sun
The Angel at the Gate

Poetry:
Fetish
Eternity to Season

HEARTLAND

WILSON HARRIS

INTRODUCTION BY MICHAEL MITCHELL

P E E P A L   T R E E

First published in Great Britain in 1964
by Faber and Faber
Republished in 2009 by
Peepal Tree Press Ltd
17 King's Avenue
Leeds LS6 1QS
England

ISBN13: 9781845230968

 Peepal Tree gratefully acknowledges Arts Council support

For Margaret,
Alf and Jean Edwards
and
Sydney Singh

The rocks will melt, the sealed horizons fall and the places
Our hearts have hid in will be viewed by strangers.

EDWIN MUIR

… being the sacrifice of the substitute within the personality, in order to rebuild the heroic image in other minds; for the impact, in the perpetual ceremony of renewal, of conflicts beyond imagination.

G. R. LEVY *The Sword From the Rock*

CONTENTS

AUTHOR'S PREFACE

THE HEARTLAND TRILOGY

Heartland, *Tumatumari* and *The Sleepers of Roraima* open doors in nature and psyche, in lands, forests, rivers, seas and a responsive imagination, to bring a psychological originality into what is a half-ruined, violent humanity. The psychology of originality is a quantum issue. A line that is fired divides mysteriously into two. Such in brief is quantum physics. I have used those two lines to suggest that one brings back ghostly features of the past we tend to forget. These quantum ghosts may be sensed in *Heartland* in that they bring back features from *Palace of the Peacock* and *The Far Journey of Oudin*. Tumatumari is a waterfall in the Potaro River, Guyana. It is an Amerindian expression which means "sleeping rocks", rocks sculpted by nature as if by the genius of man. We may therefore draw up into ourselves something of the cruelties inflicted by man upon man across ages of conquest and desolation if we are not to deceive ourselves afresh about the hollow present and future in which we remain subject to ceaseless conflicts that take many forms and guises to ape what we have forgotten. Volumes are written into nature and psyche to address the subconscious and unconscious with phases of the complex, largely undiscovered originality of a true consciousness.

Wilson Harris
4 May, 2008

9

INTRODUCTION

MICHAEL MITCHELL

Wilson Harris's novel *Heartland* begins with a spellbinding evocation of morning on one of the great rivers of the interior of Guyana. The reader is immediately struck by the physicality of the descriptions, of the river with its half-submerged rocks, broad reaches reflecting the changing sky, and the menacing draw of the rapids, or of the forest whose impenetrable depths become sources of insight and awe. It should not be underestimated what effect being alone in such a vast forest, full of inexplicable sounds in the long darkness of the night, can have, in terms of psychological disorientation and fear. It is not surprising that the protagonist, Stevenson, finds the certainties he has previously entertained suddenly dissolve.

The programmatic opening of the novel is simultaneously an ironic reversal of the process which takes place in the course of the book, and thus offers a clue to understanding Harris's unique treatment of landscape. The insubstantial mist, described as "solid", gives way to an "illusion", in which the rocks in the river appear to be swimmers surrounded by snakes. Only the full light reveals their prosaic existence. Stevenson, the focal point of the narrative here, is relieved to be able to see the landscape in terms of a "convention of perfect lifelessness" (p. 21). Although

Stevenson would like to see things, and people, in this purely conventional and objective way, he is forced throughout the novel to entertain all the possibilities which his "unreliable" senses, and the resources of the language, present to him.

Heartland is anchored, like so much of Harris's work, in a particular sense of place. When it was written, few of his readers would have travelled to the interior of Guyana, though Harris knew it well from his years as a government surveyor. Now it is accessible to tourists, who fly over the rainforest from the narrow coastal strip, with its neat grids of streets and its sugar plantations, towards the escarpment where they visit the Kaieteur Falls plunging to the valley below, before flying on to where the forest suddenly ends in the sweep of savannahs across to the Brazilian border. Even for those whose journey is only virtual, an internet satellite map clearly shows the branching Cuyuni river through the rapids below Upper Kamaria, and its passage on towards Bartica, where it joins the mighty Essequibo flowing out to the sea. It is indeed in the heart of the country, though many on the populated coastlands will never have been there.

Stevenson, too, has come there from the coast, and it is initially an alien place. He has come as the result of financial collapse and his father's death, for which, at first, he would like to believe he is blameless. Gradually, however, he begins to discover that a web of connections binds him to the fraud and deceit as well as to the apparently selfless actions of the father who shares his name, and his own involvement with his mistress Maria, the wife of the fraudster. It appears to him that the death of his father represents the death of his body as the flight of Maria is the flight of his soul.

His position at this point, a denial of responsibility and unawareness of the interconnected dynamics of the social and physical worlds, resembles that of the poet in Dante's *Divine Comedy*, from which the epigraph of Book One is taken. Lost in the wood, the poet is guided through the successive realms of the spirit and forced to see how they are structured as well as the patterns of interaction and responsibility which Dante was trying to comprehend. Over all of Dante's work there hovers the idea of the muse, and the word recurs often in Harris's novel, sometimes in this sense of soul-guide, sometimes as the spur of creativity, and sometimes in the sense of "musing", allowing the mind to open to unexpected sources of inspiration.

Stevenson has become a watchman over his company's machinery, as he believes. When he meets Kaiser, who is driving a lorry, he points out that: "this is an age of mechanical progress" (p. 28). And yet, through the course of the novel, he is removed ever further from such evidence of technology, losing even his boat, and forced to follow an "ancient line" through the rainforest or risk penetrating where there are no markers or pathways at all. His name, Stevenson, recalls the famous engineer of the steam age, and connects him with the engineer Fenwick in Harris's earlier novel *The Secret Ladder*. At the same time, bearing in mind that the protagonist of his first novel, *The Palace of the Peacock*, bore the name of a writer, we should not forget that a Stevenson was the author of that classic study of the dual nature of the human psyche, *Dr Jekyll and Mr Hyde*.

The other characters, too, bring associations from elsewhere. Kaiser, who looks cinder-black and whose clothes have the appearance of ash, shares a name with the brother burnt in a rum-shop fire in *The Far Journey of Oudin*, while daSilva, the pork-knocker whose rations Kaiser has brought, admits his identity with one of the crew who sailed with Donne. Petra, the Amerindian woman pursued by her tribe on her journey from the savannahs to have the baby which may be Donne's or daSilva's, bears a significant resemblance to the Amerindian woman Mariella in *The Palace of the Peacock*. She is also, through her name, related to the rocks and bones of the land, and, as Stevenson begins to realize, to his mistress Maria, both names of religious significance. Her baby will be the result of the transgression of boundaries which may prove to have saving potential. Harris has described these characters as "quantum ghosts". Harris takes the destabilization of the fixed categories of existence that are revealed in quantum physics, combined with the property of ghosts to reveal their presence and the trace of their previous lives, in order to allow characters to become enmeshed in time with ancient history, across barriers of race, class, wealth and gender, but also across the barriers of what would otherwise appear, in a linear history, to be borders of reality, delineated by causality. Thus he is able to open a door into revisionary "rehearsals" in which alternative realities and possibilities allow scope for the depths of judgement and the heights of redemption.

This may be why the characters bring with them some of the riddling and laconic quality of dream, with its mixture of jesting conversational familiarity and an almost archaic tone of myth. These living ghosts are figures of the unconscious – not the personal unconscious of private memories, but the collective unconscious – where they resonate beyond themselves in ways they themselves find surprising, and connect in alien familiarity with some hidden presence in the reader.

DaSilva himself expounds a fantastic philosophy which Kaiser suggests is to be expected of pork-knockers (lone prospectors for gold in the depths of the rainforest) – a kind of bewildering genius that can indeed be found in unexpected places in Guyana. This philosophy is important enough for daSilva to become the narrative focus in Chapter Six. There, in the description of the dog which takes on its companion's sickness and, in dying, cures him, there is an illustration of a pre-Enlightenment way of thinking which has become lost to Western rationalism: the idea of connection by meaning, based on analogy and association. Until the advent of quantum physics, such notions had come to be dismissed as crankishly absurd, and yet it is precisely these principles which are the source of creativity, imagination and wit, and which language, used with indeterminacy, imagery and contradictory poetry, is able to maintain and preserve as a dwindling ration in our familiar, rational world. So it should come as no surprise that Harris uses these very resources of language in describing the "patient trial and duty of ourself" (as daSilva puts it (p. 51)) undergone by his characters.

But it is landscape, in the first instance, the heart of the land, which draws the reader into an appreciation of language. This is particularly well illustrated in Chapter Two, where Stevenson plunges into the trackless jungle, believing that he has heard a movement of someone watching him. Anyone who is unfamiliar with Harris's work is likely to become as disorientated by the tangled profusion of the writing at this point as Stevenson himself is. However, closer attention to the strands of metaphor and hints of imagery will reveal organic structures where nothing is superfluous or wasted. They connect the land, with its mineral, animal and human elements, to the plan of the novel as a whole, transforming the watchers (centres of observing consciousness) into the watched (consciousness aware of its unconscious background) and finally into the creation of the watch (a fictional instrument allowing vision to be represented in a temporal narrative).

When Stevenson first leaves the clearing he perceives that: "An eye or two, like fire, had succeeded in penetrating the layers of the jungle to accentuate the absent skull of the retreating sun" (p. 39). This image of sunlight through the trees suggests a journey into the body, which he needs to make to find the heart. The whole of the land thus becomes a living body, so we find corporeal imagery everywhere: of limbs, arms, shoulders, wrists. At the same time, under the forest canopy, the world seems submarine and fluid, home to creatures that are indeterminate as to whether they are scaled or feathered. These images are repeated in the recollection of the shamanic dress of the original inhabitants seeking to find harmony with the heartland which even they had already lost. They were followed by pre-Columbian and then European colonizers, also in search of some mysterious El Dorado, although they themselves were unsure whether to define their goal as monetary gold or the golden age.

This sense of a continuum extending from the inorganic through living forms to human history and aspiration makes it clear that Harris is going far beyond an exploration of the psyche of individual characters; it is a novel of ideas, some of which strike us as being way ahead of their time. Harris is introducing his English-speaking readers to a vision of ecological and philosophical interdependence preserved within Amerindian societies but only now being rediscovered, belatedly, by our consumer cultures. The ideas, however, never come across as mere abstractions. They are embodied in a tactile, sensual world like that which Stevenson is now immersed in.

This area, at the heart of the psyche, is a dangerous place of madness and malaise, dancing to a "compulsive baton", and it is only with difficulty that Stevenson manages to re-emerge. At one point he feels like a fallen branch trapped and spread-eagled like a crucified man. Later in the novel daSilva will be hit by a falling branch and will die trapped in the rocks of a ravine like a giant coffin. The associative qualities of the language point towards a quantum identity between them. Stevenson, however, by contorting himself through the metaphorical forms of animals, and grounding himself by the miraculous blossoming of a stick in the ground, both a real stick with a tattered bit of his shirt clinging to it and the mystical Glastonbury rose, synthesizing spirit and organic nature, he is able to extricate himself and retrieve time. The scales of his instinctive experience fall from his eyes. The journey into the heartland of the unconscious needs to be redeemed in the vision of consciousness.

If the reader understands, then, that simile or metaphor does not involve one illusory term that embellishes or clarifies a realistic state or action, but is itself an equivalent and immanent reality, it is possible to read the book in a different and more productive way. The interrelatedness of the land and characters will become clearer. It will be possible to follow Stevenson as he becomes midwife to Petra's child, but with an awareness that her subsequent disappearance, with the potential conceived by the intercourse between cultures, is only the beginning of a search which Harris was to continue through the remarkable series of novels that were to follow.

BOOK ONE

THE WATCHERS

In the midway of this our mortal life,
I found me in a gloomy wood, astray
Gone from the path direct.

DANTE

I

The solid morning mist began to disintegrate and dark shoulders of rock appeared in the water giving the illusion of swimmers, reaching from bank to bank, dispersing from themselves wreaths of snakes with imperceptible strokes. But slowly it grew clear with the brightening light that the swimmers were actually stationary and the chained commotion of the stream was their deceptive gesture... Stevenson unexpectedly felt an irrational shock of fear, suffocating and dense. He drew in his breath involuntarily and held it deeply as if to preserve himself from drowning, telling himself at the same time he was a fool. His mind began to clear under his own tide of suspension and self-rebuke and his spirit lifted, restoring to the world the convention of perfect lifelessness associated with the landscape of the earth. . . .

It was a relief to return to this safe and normal ground of consciousness once again. Nevertheless, he could not entirely shake off something emotional and disturbing which had momentarily overwhelmed him like a wave out of the sun. It was the first time this had happened to him – as far back as he could remember – and certainly never before in the weeks he had spent as a watchman on the wood grant above the Kamaria falls.

The river was easily fifteen hundred feet wide at the section where he stood. He began to indulge in the ritual calculations of the area he had come to know by heart.

There was an uninterrupted view across the water save for the sculptured backs of stone appearing here and there. The springs of turbulence which coiled around the rocks where the current seemed to spark and divide heralded the imminent break-up of the stream into several channels and islands. The race for the rapids was about to begin. Stevenson could hear the distant roar of the falls like a great electric crowd poised in space to witness an event. Nevertheless he knew he was alone with the spectre of the forest. It was a thought which, without reason, it was becoming difficult to measure and contain. . . .

He unwound a length of rope from the tree-stump to which his dinghy had been moored, seated himself in the stern and with a deft movement propelled and paddled the nervous craft into the grasp of the tide. The torn skin of the water began to hiss, and the bones of the river acquired a new threatening disposition chained within the uneven moods of the sky. The open reflection at the landing was fast turning into a jagged accumulation of elements, half-air, half-earth, vegetation and shadow and stone, all staggering to make a larger, more solid still, unearthly presence than ever before. A hanging profile materialized at last and Stevenson glided upon a giant's suspended tongue, seventy-five feet wide, licking the opposite bank of the river and leaving a delicate bubbling trail along a continuous knife-edge of leaves. . . . At last the eternal tone of the falls seemed to slice into its own heart and volume so that it was possible for one to distinguish in the echoing roots of the forest a clear and yet profound trailing note and Stevenson strained his attention to catch the disembodied branches of hiss and roar, the strangest aerial sublimations of bitterness and cruelty, apprehended vaguely time and time again in numerous, often abrupt, veins and shades of sound across mediating distances. . . .

The singular, agonizing thread of time declined and he was aware only of a smothering tumult of expression. The dangerous descent of the rapids was still at least half a mile away but it seemed to lie in the very passage of water under his feet. . . .

There was a sudden indentation in the bank, the over-hanging forest began to recede a little and a clearing burst into view; he dug with his paddle and ran the dinghy on to a landing, sprang out and fastened the anchor chain to a pole.

The land rose and, as he expected, on gaining the com-mencement of the jungle road and portage – constructed to by-pass the Kamaria falls – he came upon a lorry parked beside a small weather-beaten depot. He called – "Kaiser. Kaiser." No one answered. He raised his voice again until his shout seemed to climb and strike the wall of sunlit trees in the rear of the clearing and return to the ground like the desiccated echo of a falling branch. He addressed the light and the shadow around him once more and watched and listened, so anxious for the particular human cry he needed, he actually grew deaf to the train of explosive noises which distinguished the bush so that they were reduced in his mind to a muffled passage of innumerable artificial insects on wires punctuated by feathered bells. He returned to the animate life of himself and his surroundings with a start and shouted at the top of his voice, listening and watching as before so exclusively and intently for the presence of Kaiser that the crowded rapids of both forest and river settled again into a dumb atrophied explosion and silent roar.

He turned around and stared unseeingly at – hating and loving at the same time – the waterway of the channel which had opened out a little beneath him between the island of consciousness and the stable ground where he now stood. Island and mainland occupied positions approximating to fantasy and reality and it was as if he knew he both needed and feared to manufacture for himself such models of aloof security, while driven to an extreme appreciation of the living value and danger in the self-created responses of their material fellowship. . . . The crude portage ran for five to six miles further downriver through the bush and stopped at the foot of the falls. It was an invaluable mode of transport which saved one from facing the long series and the intensity of the rapids on the rivertop. The government, as a matter of fact, Stevenson mused (and he regretfully contemplated the loss of a fascinating and empirical mental prospect) had expressly forbidden the way through the falls since many lives and much property, barrels of food and personal possessions had gone down in the old days. . . . Kaiser lived in the combined resthouse, garage and base camp at the foot of the falls. He was the driver and overseer of the lorry parked on the road and responsible for bringing cargo up from Lower Kamaria for distribution from the depot at Upper Kamaria to the scattered company or companies of men, explorers and miners, pork-knockers as they were sometimes called, strung out topside along the river as far as, or even beyond, who could tell, Devil's Hole rapids of Venezuela. . . .

Stevenson's speculative frontiers collapsed with a rude shout from Kaiser and he turned abruptly. The man was here at last. Stevenson could never stop being curious every time he saw Kaiser, as if he wanted to confirm that this must be the strangest, most haunting or haunted creation of all things and beings he visualized. It was not merely the blackness of Kaiser's skin, within whose flesh appeared incandescent eyes lit as from the density of coal. It was the ghostly ash of the garments he wore; a breath of wind would surely have dispersed them, the most attenuated vest and shorts Stevenson had ever seen, plucked in the nick of time, he was inclined to swear, from some ancient fire.

Everything about the man possessed this scorched self-sufficiency, involuntarily self-creative as it was self-corrective, as pathetic, since apparently self-inflicted, as it was admirable, since apparently the inherent design of all nature, crumbling and yet enduring all the time and giving him both the stamp of continuous frailty and the glance or passion of immaterial conviction or immunity from death. What an extraordinary and impulsive idea. Stevenson grew ashamed and afraid, not of Kaiser in truth but of his own unreliable senses – if one looked at life in this dubious way – which were capable of playing exceptional tricks upon him, or if he looked otherwise – with religious fear – of invoking a sensibility akin to a phenomenon of all-inclusive agency and humility, vindicating and confirming past, present and future lives and therefore pointing to a community of conscious fulfilment in existence.

Kaiser was depositing within his lorry the gun he had been carrying over his shoulder. "Not a blasted creature today," he grumbled. "It's the engine of this damned lorry scaring away mankind's good game. What on earth can we do? Tell me that, Mr. Stevenson. I was a rich landowner and a teacher some years ago but I lose every-thing in a fire – life and a degree of fortune —" he laughed at his manner of symbolic expression – "and I finding since then that I got to begin to learn to live and to help others live on next to nothing. . . ." There was an ironical jesting smile on his raw burnt-looking lips which infused his expression with the instinctive realization that Stevenson needed – out of consuming self-interest – someone else in the bush whose image and whose help-less confession and speech he could relate to his own and every man's being. . . . The sun was beginning to spread its brilliant chaotic canvas upon the river and down every vague skylight and well of forest, not only upon the high dense refractive carpet that roofed the jungle but in the insubstantial spirit of a mural floating deep within perceptive valleys and rising areas of ground. . . .

Stevenson moved closer to the lorry and stood in the shadow of the depot. "Better luck next time Kaiser." He spoke solicitously without, however, really caring, he was so preoccupied. Then he voiced the real question – "Are you coming over this way again tomorrow?"

"Not tomorrow. Maybe daSilva will be along though. Keep an eye out for him."

"DaSilva! Never heard of him."

Kaiser gave a chuckle. "You ain't been in the bush long, that's plain. Funniest pork-knocking guy in the world daSilva is. Call *me* a spook but he looks like death itself. The stories circulating in this river! You can't pin a soul down in the end." He laughed both at himself and at daSilva. "Imagine *me* calling another man the funniest guy in the world . . . ." He broke off all at once and began to stare more closely than ever at Stevenson. "Nothing I say seem to have any joy in it for you today, Mr. Stevenson. You look sad and serious as a stick. Anything gone wrong?"

"Oh, I'm right as rain," Stevenson protested, glancing up at the brilliant sky. He felt a faint inward cold tremor, starting as a prickling branch at the top of his spine and glancing into fireworks of sensible warmth. The spasmodic sensation enveloped the rooted flesh of his back and passed. "I didn't sleep too well last night though," he confessed, "and I've been having the most absurd thoughts all morning." He tried to laugh.

Kaiser's burning eyes opened wide and flickered – "You ain't too deep in a scare at being left all alone in the jungle, is you?" His voice grated with the mournful

26

rhythm the body of a tree makes when it cracks with the wind, seeming to deplore the inadequacy of language itself – the conventional force and unconventional weight-less origin of a self one half-remembers, half-forgets with a startled groan.

Stevenson tried to make a joke in the face of Kaiser's grotesque concern – "I know you're versed in the art of how to withstand the crack of doom, Kaiser." He half-laughed as he spoke. "It's consoling to know you're around; and now you've told me of the presence of this daSilva you obviously admire" – the timbre of his voice had grown mocking and inquisitorial – "it makes me feel almost human again. The truth is sometimes I can't endure the thought of being absolutely alone. It would be ridiculous in the circumstances anyway, wouldn't it? Why would I need to be here then at all?" He stopped on a note of exasperation and Kaiser regarded him slyly. Stevenson wanted to throw by the horns the bull of subversion and anxiety he inwardly faced. He hated the change which was sweeping over him. He had begun secretly to deplore the pedantic image of self-importance and suspicion he was used to advertising to the world, when driven by ancient psychological habit to establish and reinforce the obses-sive validity of his occupation or job, however meaning-less and empty this was. "Surely there must be others," he insisted, "in this part of the bush, the bad ones of society"– his face looked guilty – "or why would I be here at all, I ask you again, as a highly paid watchman? I tell you what"– he declared impulsively – "I shall become manager of the grant one day, if it ever gets going as it should. And so in the meantime it's up to me to grin and bear it, the isolation and all that" – his voice grew forced and belligerent – "and see that no son-of-a-gun takes it into his scheming head to pinch a few handy pieces of the company's expensive machinery. Believe me, some of it's worth just as much and some a damn sight more than this." He gave the fender of Kaiser's lorry a hard slap. "This is an age of mechanical progress, Kaiser." He looked threatening now – "It's no use denigrating that. Every fool has got to see or it's all up with them."

"Are you sure?" Kaiser asked with the air of one who was scarcely listening.

"Course I am. . . ."

"I didn't mean *that*." Kaiser lifted his hand and gave the fender of the lorry his own blow of fate. "I mean how you come to be so sure you ain't standing alone in this forest of a world – as you're already inclined to suspect – and no one's there in *person* – truly good or bad – for you to watch? You sure your business of somebody needing to steal *machinery*" – he spoke with a measure of disdain – "ain't just a dead or premature invention?"

"Of course I'm sure. . . ." Stevenson stopped, confronted and deeply shocked by the game of self-parody he sometimes believed he had invented, and the annihilation of personal responsibility and freedom of choice. The trouble was he had never learnt to surrender himself to a true vocation, dialectical or spiritual (though all his dealings rested on the gamble of history and the boast of a continuity of mind) and therein lay – in the lapse of this core of an open awareness – the imprisonment of obsessed and frustrated being. He rejected the startling bitter judgement with embarrassment. It sprang from, he tried to convince himself, the ghostly infection of nerves which was making him confusedly aware how bankrupt and devoid of reserves he was in the past and incapable of discovering a motive or hand of distinction in himself.

"Where's this man daSilva?" he cried wishing to divert his thoughts.

"Pork-knocking anywhere between Matope and Devil's Hole . . . ." Kaiser's reply was laconic but full of commiseration.

"How far is Matope from here?"

"Ten to fifteen miles roughly." Kaiser lifted a burnt cautionary finger – "Don't go looking though. Like searching for a needle in a haystack to find daSilva in the bush. And it's a full day, or even more, paddling against the stream to reach Matope. You'd lose your job too if your principals find out you left your post for as long as that."

"To hell with my principals. Why is daSilva coming to Kamaria?"

Kaiser pointed towards the depot. "A skimpy supply of rations come for him from Bartica town. Just enough to keep body and soul together. Tell him when you see him pass your landing tomorrow that I put his ration boxes in there and I place the key of the depot in the usual hiding place." He could not help glancing involuntarily around to see no one was about before he parted a large drooping flag of grass behind which a key had been cleverly concealed in a crevice of the building.

Stevenson was unable to resist being sceptical. "I wish to God I honestly knew from whom you're hiding the key, Kaiser. There's nobody in his right senses who would bore the bush and go to the trouble of stealing poor daSilva's miserable food. It's scarcely worth a dime, is it?"

"How you know daSilva's pennywise ration ain't worth more than all the millionaire hardware in the world to a starving wild devil of a man who don't give a damn for a thing?" Kaiser slapped the long-suffering fender of the lorry with violence.

Stevenson was unable to reply and Kaiser turned away to brood – ashamed of his loss of control – fastening his eyes upon the black shapeless canvas shoes – torn by all weathers

– he wore, as if he saw an ambiguous countenance residing in a half-world of creation and invention. Which was which and what was what? he wondered. He began to exercise the flexible tip of his shoe like a brush with which he painted broad strokes and lines on the ground.

"What are you digging away there for?" Stevenson demanded.

"Trying to find me self-portrait," Kaiser looked up. "Is something I feel one can never be sure of. . . ."

Stevenson was exasperated. "The trouble with you Kaiser is that the only damned thing you're ever sure of is the rag-and-bone reality of this world."

Kaiser indulged in his raw jesting smile. He began to erase – with the sole of his boot – the fragmentary portrait he had drawn. "I believe in every crumb of fulfilment I bring," he said matter-of-factly at last, hoping this would establish a legitimate vocation and excuse for being. But Stevenson could not help growing incensed. "Crumb of fulfilment?" he mocked. "Rubbish. I won't accept such a trick." He looked all at once like a blind man. "Yes – it's just a trick of the senses I've been entertaining this morning and I won't let it seduce me any longer. It's the craziest idea on earth. . . ." he stopped. "Or is it?" His face was torn by a terrible conflict.

Kaiser's flickering eyes glowed savagely for a moment with the light of protest but he closed them at last with an effort and his features acquired repose. "Nobody can be sure how much store – more than you and me dream – it means to them. . . ." His voice was muffled coming from an uncertain depth.

"Them who?" Stevenson broke into crude mimicry of the dialogue of the folk.

"Why, beggars and pork-knockers like daSilva! You need them and they need you like skin need bone. Man need man, Mr. Stevenson." Kaiser's eyes opened and flared and surveyed the flag of grass behind which the paradoxical key of all substance he guarded was hidden.

It was this sobering reflection which gave Stevenson the moral desire to remain at his post: he was beginning to grow aware – however much he tried to suppress it – of the fact that he possessed little more in the past than a body of prejudice upon which he always counted for a driving coherency and economic force.

The initial shock to this self-assurance came a year ago, long before he dreamt of coming to Kamaria, though at the time, when the disaster occurred, it did not spell for him an immediate and crushing nervous reaction. *Now* he was becoming sensitive – in a way he never before was – to the ultimatum which resides in economic circumstance and in the death of one's fortunes. Nothing short of such a substantial loss could have been instrumental in provoking him to gamble with visionary resources for a spiritual chance. How did he come to take such an extreme and quixotic step? Indeed the choice of the heartland had not been his. . . until *now*. . . for what had really started in an accident and the pursuit of mere expediency was only now, today, in process of confirming itself in retrospect as his own grave stake and risk. Would this come to mean for him in the future the accumulative fulfilment of all the blind folly of the past, or would it bring him the conscious reality of a true grain of wisdom? Would he be confronted finally by an impossibility of escaping from himself, living or dead, or would he discover an identity of abandonment which would inform him and sometimes lead him like his own shadow into the subtlest realization of time?

When the crash came, a year or so ago, everyone said Stevenson was callous, appearing as he did so indifferent to the blow of fate which was to shock his father into despair. That was not true, Stevenson himself knew. His indifference sprang from a certain hardness, yes, but it was the hardness of a bitter optimism, deeply felt, an involuntary core of refusal to accept a total reversal of fortune. He was genuinely unable to credit the notion of overwhelming loss or defeat; his instinct was that of a born gambler, over-inclined to be sceptical of a self-sufficient mode of fortune, and naturally, or unnaturally, as one chose to think, disposed to explore every fleeting vein of unconditional attachment to privilege and servitude. His father was often horrified by this economic heresy and the threat it posed to a secure order of life and had even threatened, on one occasion, to change his will drastically. No wonder he could not share with his son the base capacity to insulate himself – at the time of the disaster – from the crushing effects of absolute misfortune. It may have been heartless indifference or just a curious short-circuit of nervous reaction but whatever it was it helped Stevenson to set out for the interior with fewer qualms than he would have otherwise endured. He responded to the empirical necessity of doing something to scrape together a livelihood but he was still oblivious to the gravity of his situation. Which was just as well, as if he had understood what was happening to him *then,* and what lay before him *now,* he may have despaired of making the smallest effort. There was irony in all this for it was his worthless feature, unfeeling and despicable in the eyes of the world, which gave him the measure of buoyancy he possessed like an unconscious and ignoble state of the soul making for an insubstantial premise; and this counted for all when all that seemed to matter was lost. . . . It was this trait of the gambler which moved him like a weak and perverse but invaluable impulse, more daring and extraordinary than he dreamed. . . .

It was equally extraordinary (when one stopped to think of it) what a safe umbrella over him his father's reputation had been. He grew up taking this for granted like an act of nature but in actual fact it represented a considerable personal achievement, based on scrupulous business dealings and the exercise of responsibilities rooted in foreign as well as domestic concerns. The stature his father achieved exacted its own infallible penalty by making room for failure a vulgar impossibility. It was a stooping, mournful, albeit dignified, figure Stevenson recalled and – for the first conscience-stricken time – he wondered what pride and horror his father may have secretly entertained. The dark weathered features sometimes gave the illusion of being drained of all colour, and the domed (or was it *doomed)* forehead and brow – Stevenson pondered, squinting high at the Kamaria sun – was invariably marked with a stiff frown.

On other occasions the face seemed to change – to grow brownish and cracked like the bark of a tree; a single black mole would emerge and cling like a curious insect to the flaked skin high on the bone of one cheek. . . .

(Stevenson turned and stared along the dark hallucinated corridor of the portage – his eyes were black from the glance of the sun – where Kaiser had driven the lorry and vanished. It was not long since he had driven away and the whine of the gears could be heard only a short moment ago as the motor ascended a hill. The sound seemed to blend, as he listened again, into the falling thud and throb of the rapids, and into a concert of engines – self-created and universal – neither of which could be purely distinguished from each other.)

Stevenson had often been told he looked like a younger version of his father's image. He recalled now – with all the shattering poignancy of growing awareness from which he had been guarded in the past, as the seed is protected by its mask of earth – the aged and still ageless countenance belonging to his house of ancestors. He may have misjudged the ordeal and necessity in his father's reserve as he, too, was misjudged in his own appearance of unfeeling spirit. They shared an antagonism of relatedness which supported the open and closed nature of the community of the world like the shutters of a camera or the disposition of eye and lid. . . .

The question, which now arose with a force it had never before possessed, was – did Zechariah Stevenson engineer protection for his son (and namesake too) who would have been charged – if it had not been for his father's likely intervention – with conspiracy to defraud the company of which he was director? Large-scale defalcations had come to light and Zechariah Stevenson, jnr., it was discovered, was an intimate friend of the young Brazilian wife of Bernard Camacho, middle-aged, trusted accountant employed by Zechariah, snr. Camacho had been on a normal round of Caribbean stations when he broke away into Latin America with a large sum at his fingertips. This was the last stroke – an examination of his books revealed – in a masterly series of fraudulent practice which no one, until then, had dreamed to detect. . . .

The news was kept a religious secret from everyone save the highest authorities in the firm and it only became widely known when Zechariah Stevenson vanished from the deck of the steamer plying between Demerara and Pomeroon. His body was washed up a couple of days later high on the Pomeroon foreshore of Jigsaw Bay. . . .

Stevenson had scarcely begun to digest the news of the terrible event when he learnt for the first time about Camacho and the major fraud which had been perpetrated on the company. He tried to reach his mistress, Maria Camacho, on the telephone and discovered – to his astonishment –

that she, too, had fled and was – at that very moment – on a plane for Rio where she intended to disembark *en route* for an unknown destination. She had flown out of Demerara early that morning and Stevenson was dumbfounded for she had dropped no hint to him whatsoever. He wanted to curse her for practising such deception but was unable to express even the fact that she had gone away for good. *She must return to him sooner or later, she was necessary to him. . . .* Nevertheless the combination of disclosures and effects stunned him and reduced him to a stoical fit, a mood of stubborn inapprehension, a refusal to bow to the passage of events which his colleagues misinterpreted as callous indifference to thwarted fortune and thwarted romance. They were not surprised that he appeared equally unimpressed by the fact that his father – in the week at his disposal before the announcement of the scandal – had drawn up a deed of surrender of all sums and sources of his private savings to repair the depredations inflicted upon shareholders whose interests he felt he must protect. Could it be, Stevenson now wondered, that they had believed him to be indifferent to the loss of everything because they reckoned he knew it was the price his father had paid to save him? What a totally ridiculous assumption. Surely they must *know* he was innocent. Indeed this was the truth, he swore. He recalled the disdain he had felt when there had been threatening talk of a charge of conspiracy to defraud being preferred against him. The rumour, however, came to nothing within a week of his father's death. What deal, if any, had old Zechariah made with his colleagues which they now respected?

It was a fantastic and baseless notion. Nevertheless it began to haunt him like a bargain of ghostly events flitting through his mind so that for the first time he began to appreciate the ordeal and misery and shock of his father's life, the great unnatural sacrifice involved in the preservation of the last shreds of dignity. His father's death, in this moment of nervous and blinding illumination, became *his,* and the endeavour to fulfil and save a certain presence, a certain priceless achievement in the past, became his also. In gambling with everything, he had been involuntarily leading the older man to the point where he too surrendered everything. The opposition they offered each other – which had been bitter at times – was also an unconscious way of vindicating each other.

Stevenson was growing acutely aware of the terror and distress at the centre of his life, so much so that he spoke aloud to himself, insisting he was innocent of an attempt to defraud anyone, whatever anybody may have thought. And yet had he not been guilty of an affair with Maria, whereby he may have lightly and thoughtlessly divulged top confidential pieces of information gleaned from his father, which she may have passed on to her husband? How could he be absolutely certain he had not contributed to a network of conspiracy like a spider's web on which light and shade danced together like etchings within a phenomenal mirror of wood? A frightful screen of inward recollection like the sunlight and shadows of a dead still world (there was not a breath of air in the lifeless forest) began to assemble and lend itself to reflecting the opaque consciousness and stream of fact. Did illusion and reality truly lend themselves to the recreation of an incredible self-portrait in order to provide a distinction between the works of arrogance and the works of faith? He had acutely jeopardized his own integrity and his father's not only by his intimacy with Maria but by continuing to defend her blindly, when she fled, in order to avoid shouldering or accepting the notion of her treachery. It was his pride which was at stake, not her virtue, and therefore he insisted with every breath that she was a victim of circumstances. He was adamant that she had not betrayed the understanding they had had (no doubt as his father had been determined to shield him from criminal charges).

Father and son both gambled all the time on the slenderest thread of universal and practical reason, the ultimate rejection of damaging misconduct in favour of a constructive propriety informed, firstly, by the impeccable record of the past (one could draw upon), secondly, by elementary compassion, after all, since beauty such as Maria's always brought with it a certain licence to make inroads on conviction as well as convention. This was eminently natural and surely the world of growing liberal proportions would arrive at the wisdom of closing its ranks around misdemeanours of the muse of the soul. Was it idealism or perversity, self-interest or spirituality, to nurse the extremity of reconciliation and hope? To hope against hope for the miracle of being?

In some strange way he had never accepted his father's death until that death was in process of becoming *his,* just as he had never accepted Maria's flight as genuine until he, too, began to lose and betray himself. *The death of his body and the flight of his soul were now becoming real. . . .* Once again Stevenson was shaken by his absurd and terrifying new-found response to a corpus of tradition or belief he sought both to abandon and entertain. . . . It was still possible at this moment to misconceive dreadfully another's motive or intention, and this ambivalence and uncertainty charged him afresh to recreate an act of meaningful self-destruction wherein *he* (in recollecting his father's death) began to renounce the overwhelming scandal involved in the trial and judgement of the world. . . . He turned and stared at the door behind which Kaiser said he had left daSilva's rations – like an offering and token to an obscure god – and the barren fear grew in him that he might be inwardly consenting to an improvident trick which dispossessed him of everything and everyone tran-

37

scendental and there might be nothing at all within the storehouse of the heartland.

2

The fear he now possessed was shapeless and nameless. It was as strong and as weak as the fluid constitution of man, it was a channel for the pitiful and pitiless senses, it was equally an organ of spirit as of humiliating inconsistency and reverberating anticlimax. It was the universal and faltering choir of dead voices in living and living voices in dead. . . . A breeze was rising in the forest and the conjunctive voice of the waterfall began to change its note and pitch. Stevenson put his hands to his ears. The muffled voluminous roar followed him, intimate as the porous texture of the sun and the wind; his skin grew into breathing shreds of paper supported by wire, which possessed an irritating nib or splinter like a tick embedded in the flesh on his chest. He dug the fiendish instrument out and crushed it upon the nail on each thumb like something which was maliciously alive. A thin mark remained on the naked parchment of his body, a half-formed letter beginning to disappear already under the exposure of the elements. Stevenson fastened his shirt again and glanced up into the sky.

It was an hour past noon and he was aware, even at this early hour, of the premature settlement of the night in the strange inward growing gloom of the forest. He, too, was growing jealous of the relative clearing of the day he possessed as the night advanced and he sought to rivet himself to the brilliant flakes and chunks of light which speckled the skin of the ground.

Far away he could hear what sounded like the hiss of rain falling on the tops of the trees. The vegetation in the clearing began to respond and quiver with a startled sympathetic commotion and the flag of grass Kaiser had indicated earlier gave a sprinkled lurch like a horse's mane. Stevenson leaned forward, parting the wild growth to insert his finger in the grinning crevice of the wall before him. He removed the key and was on the point of unlocking the depot when there was a sharp splintering crack like a dry branch underfoot. He sprang to attention and turned. Two dozen or so paces away was the gloomy corridor of the portage and if anyone happened to be there in the shadow, Stevenson knew, he would be able to *see* without being seen. He wanted desperately to reconnoitre the ground but his feet were heavy as wood. With a great effort he began to advance, consoled by the consciousness of the clearing and of the skylight he still felt on his back as he drew past the first curtain of bush.

It was less dark inside than he had imagined but nevertheless a vast twilight lay everywhere. An eye or two, like fire, had succeeded in penetrating the layers of the jungle to accentuate the absent skull of the retreating sun which seemed all at once to fall far behind. It was cool under the trees and he passed his hand along his brow where the flakes of perspiration had dried into a brittle film of dust.

Some of his fright had evaporated with the inevitability of his advance into the everlasting green vault, half-night, half-day; he slipped forward like a log in the trough and cradle of a green wave of earth. He stopped and listened, half-forgetting himself – the present idol he made of each limb – for whom and which he had been filled with such bestial and involuntary alarm.

He discerned no one and yet a short while ago he could have sworn he had distinctly heard someone's foot crack in the undergrowth. Grotesque idea. Born of the diseased imagination of the jungle, he chided himself. But the censure fell flat. It was too late to derive comfort from self-mockery. He was certain he had heard someone or something, and the mood of place he was experiencing began to sustain him in this view and to lead him into an area which promised to lie beyond both scepticism and reason for fear. He was entering the world of obsession, a climate of the mind where travellers, ancient and modern, had been ruled by a particular spell of madness which encouraged the illusion of absolute freedom from affright or else drew a chain of baffling terror around anyone who plunged, all alone, into the bush.

Nothing changed over the centuries. Long before European colonizer – Portuguese, Spanish, French, Dutch, English – and African colonized arrived and ventured into nameless tributaries, their pre-Columbian spiritual ancestors had been on the selfsame ground, Toltec or Peruvian administrators or merchants with their attendants and middlemen. They had apparently failed in their mission to catch the unreality of themselves which they encountered in the rude nomadic tribes they came to rescue and civilize, who flitted like ghosts under a more compulsive baton, born of the spirit of place, than any a human conqueror could devise. Legendary hunted creatures they all were and their legend was an extraordinary malaise, the imitative dance of beast or fish or fowl, the inspired flight of the shaman seeking god, the incredible convolvular gyration of secret bodies with fins or feathers on their heads, ending and beginning again the proliferate dance and vegetative process of life. Their religion was an extreme capacity for avenues of flight they made for themselves to discover a heartland which had been created for them and which they had lost.

But to experience their heights of intoxicated limbs was to suffer as well an acute fall into the void. The golden age they wished to find – the Palace of the Peacock – may never have existed for all anyone knew. Existence *now* was what counted. And this existence was becoming real for Stevenson, divided as it was between poles of contrary emotion which invoked confusion as to the origins of genius, the capacity for both apparent failure and success, the role of invention no one could distinguish or separate from the spirit of creation. It was this shadow of malaise which led one on continually to enter the stream of promissory unity and fulfilment. . . .

Stevenson drew himself to an abrupt halt. He recalled turning off the roadway of the portage and wandering impulsively along a pork-knocker's flickering line Kaiser himself may have cut on a recent hunting trip. It was a deceptive trail which could easily be missed if one stepped a few paces into the bush. . . . Stevenson was astonished to find he had indeed parted a large overhanding swirl of vine and lost his bearing and place. He was immersed in the directionless depth of the forest, the whispering fluid tapestry of leaves spreading and undulating amidst the adamant trunk of horned wave and branch. He stumbled through shallows of light only to find himself in the ancient bed of a dead creek. The flight of water had long ceased and turned to a desiccated allusive reflection like the bubble of stone and moss. The chained spray of branches shot and twisted from arms of rock whose handcuffed wrists half-grasped and pulled their cords and roots into the air. The jungle of the ravine led to the falls, Stevenson tried to reason; the prospect looked so impenetrable it aroused a panic of associations.

The forest was settling upon him and the offensive march of the rapids was muffled and broken by the lie of the land, seeming to turn into a subversive force underground rather than to pour from the sovereign fastness of the sky. Stevenson sank to his knees on his own fierce redoubt, assembled out of the ambivalent processes of reaction and flux. He felt partly weak, partly strong like the collapsing limb of a tree, pinned and still groping upon the floor of the ravine, subject to voluminous and obscure pressures of organic sensibility. One foot was clenched fast within the knuckled sights of a gun fashioned out of rock in a shoulder of the ravine and uplifted like the strong hand of death. Stevenson struggled to free himself from this contradiction, contorting his body even further into every alarming shape, snake and man and beast until with a spread-eagled resolution he unlocked the clasp of the rock from himself. His breath exploded with the force of the feud between form and being, matter and spirit he had been enacting. He was still unable, however, to trust the loud triumph of his senses; he nosed his way grotesquely and wildly forward, half-fish, half-reptile, through the stiff tide of the bush until his garments were ripped to scales, and a shred hooked like the tattered end of a fly on a pole with which he collided. He was forced to stop, his forehead severely bruised by the blow, feeling himself dizzily grounded by the pole or branch which now appeared tantalizingly solid and familiar, inverted by memory, upheld by the spirit of circumstance. The pole was blossoming in his consciousness. A bleached-looking flower, resembling a piece of the shirt he wore, had transferred itself to dangle – with the air of an uprooted button – from one of the rents between cloth and vest.

Stevenson stared at the thin shell of petal and the frail bait of scent rose and dwelt in his nostrils. Yes, he had held and smelt this tree before, flower as well as bark. He recalled now he had first seen it shortly before he plunged into the swirling undergrowth and sank into the ravine. The scales began to fall from his eyes. The terror subsided. A couple of paces and he knew where he was. Standing safely upon Kaiser's elusive line which started from the main portage. He held himself like a stranger as if he had been torn and stitched together again by the needle of acute personal relief. Time had been retrieved but the agonizing tenses of earth and water – the solid present and the fluid past – left him still gasping, uncertain of every living exercise, unsure whether the act of breathing was not an instinctual form of breathlessness as well.

BOOK TWO

THE WATCHED

Follow me, and I will make you fishers of men.

MATTHEW IV, 19

3

Stevenson scrambled out of the river and grabbed his towel, holding it against his body as if he felt alien eyes upon his nakedness. The head of the morning sun had risen above a fist of trees across the river. And the events of yesterday seemed almost indistinguishable from a watchful dream in the past night. Nevertheless they possessed enduring substance for him since on his return to the clearing on the river bank at Upper Kamaria – after recovering Kaiser's line – he had opened the depot and counted three or four boxes labelled *daSilva*. Kaiser had not been indulging in an idle trick or fanciful token after all. . . .

Stevenson began to dress hurriedly. He shivered a little as he stared at his reflection which grimaced and rippled in the water at his feet. He had scarcely borne remaining in the river for more than half a minute this morning. And soon, he foresaw, all he would be able to do was dip a solid bucketful and wash himself on dry land. He had never been uneasy before about swimming at the flattened foot or landing of the wood grant – where he had been stationed – as it provided an indentation like extended toes within which he kept himself safe from the open reach of the current. He told himself now his reluctance and fear sprang from his knowledge of the fluid electric eel which grazed in the dark waters hereabouts. But the truth was deeper still. It was related to the new dreadful subjective consciousness and appropriation of his father's death – the undignified extensive creature, half-human still, drowned and spread-eagled like a futile bloated animal – which was fished out of the Pomeroon on to Jigsaw Bay.

He was aroused by the sound of a paddle on the gunwale of an approaching craft. A thin reed of a voice, borne easily upon the watertop, hailed him and the glimmer of a small boat with its spidery paddling arms appeared coming from upriver. They vanished behind a rock like a bodiless trick of sunlight and then emerged, still fitful but more distinct, quickening their stroke as they came. They began to draw smoothly up to the landing, painting a smudged shadow on a wash of sun. Stevenson caught the flung line which drew him into the picture and the figure in the boat erected his long legs and came angling ashore. He looked on the verge of wrinkling himself up again and painlessly folding himself into a ball, though remaining immaculately and painfully thin; the bones in his face were like splinters and the flesh over each fragile support was turning into grey animated newspaper which preserved its texture even though its ancient print was difficult to read.

"*You* the daSilva Kaiser spoke about?" Stevenson could scarcely believe his eyes.

The man nodded. "What about a drink of coffee?" he cried. "Black and strong. I live on this for days on end." On his lips had been written such need it was almost as if a black cup were the transubstantiation of gold.

"Sure." Stevenson led the way. He felt at a loss for words. DaSilva stopped and settled himself on the first treader he encountered on the ladder mounting to Stevenson's resthouse. "When the river flood this bank, maybe a body can draw a strand of safety and comfort up there." He lifted his head quizzically to survey the resthouse which was dappled with the leaves and branches of shadow from a tall tree standing in the clearing. "But you got to be on you

48

guard all day and night long nothing don't fall on your head, even when it attacking from the bottom up." He looked penetratingly at Stevenson. "I can see you is a frightened Friday of a newcomer." He had been speaking softly but now he raised his voice. "You got to look out for wood ants as well as water, Mr. Stevenson." He passed his hand under the treader on which he sat, like a man fishing for roots in a stream he knew by heart and brought to light what looked like a desiccated catch of shells. "Yes, they're right under my ass this very moment. Wood ants' nest. You hearing me up there, Mr. Stevenson?"

Stevenson appeared at the open doorway. "Wood ants," he exclaimed indifferently, "I've got an insecticide which will exterminate them before they climb much higher. . . ." he spoke with the air of a man advertising an abstract remedy in a boring catalogue of events.

"Don't put it off too long," daSilva warned him. His woe-begone face grew sad, mocking and ludicrous and his expression turned to that of a private joker who had long grown sceptical of the public figure he cut. "A body like you must learn to follow the shadow of an ant through the needle's eye of duty. Or else you'll drown your heart in a flood of sorrow."

"Needle's eye of duty?" Stevenson was astonished. He felt himself becoming both emotionally and almost spiritu- ally involved in the pork-knocker's riddling countenance. "Where's the virtue in catching and killing a few miserable parasites. . . ?"

"Can't you see the endless virtue?" daSilva's voice fell. "I'm sure you can." He was pointing a finger at the jungle as though he had forgotten Stevenson and addressed someone else standing in the depth of the bush. Stevenson felt all at once stricken and shrunken and distressed. He recalled his plain duty to his guest and turned back indoors where a

49

kettle was now boiling. He returned bearing steaming cups of coffee and biscuits and cheese. DaSilva accepted the breakfast silently but none the less gratefully. He ate like someone ravenous, devouring the last avid crumb on his plate. At last he sighed and looked up at Stevenson. "Is a hard life, ain't it?" Stevenson nodded. "But a man must follow his duty," daSilva pontificated, "wherever it lead him, whether to something small or big. If he want to eat he must be whatever he got to be – unknown soldier or servant or saint; he may vanish underfoot or climb to a mountainous peak. Some got pleasant fields of duty to feed in, others got hard diminishing roads to walk." DaSilva's face was ludicrous and sententious and sad.

Stevenson tried to laugh. "I haven't met a goddam pork-knocker who hasn't an evangelizing itch in his mixed make-up. Some kind of megalomania. If they aren't sore about one thing, they're crazy about another. Yours is this business of duty. You remind me of my dutiful Scottish ancestors. . . ."

"You're learning to read. . . ." daSilva began. . . .

"Learning to read whom and to read what?" Stevenson's voice was rude.

DaSilva made an obsessed gesture of delineation once more which sought to scratch the universal spectre of history. He turned and gave Stevenson a critical glance. "The question is – you right to ask that – *whom* and *what*?" Stevenson tried to brush the whole inquiry aside but daSilva went on – "You getting the true inquisitorial appetite" – he rolled *inquisitorial* with ancient relish on his tongue – "for the law in the line of a thing and the unique person in the simple word of a censor. . . ."

Stevenson was both fascinated and repelled by the abrupt and fantastic logic in his visitor. "I can't say I follow. . . ." he began. DaSilva interrupted – "Is the hardest thing in the world to follow a living question in every dying rebuke and the spirit of the dead in every. . . ." He paused waiting for Stevenson to finish his sentence but Stevenson only shook the long brush of hair on his head impatiently.

"Don't worry," daSilva went on, "if life look like it riding and devouring you every day to make you extend you being longer and longer, till you find what the long line of you humanity is all about." He lowered his voice a little and glanced across the clearing into the forest as if ashamed of his hunger and emotion. "Is a kind of curse to face, maybe. But when you live like a bloody king of a pork-knocker you can't help scraping, the bottom of every barrel for a taste of ruling wisdom even if in the end you is the laughing stock of fools. So many of us cursed to live like hangers-on, parasites. What's the use of pretending we know every-thing? We got to nurse all our non-existent resources to the last bitter farthing. That's why I can't help declaring some-times" – he spoke with passion – "that it would be better if we were all finished – the greedy misconception and labour of us – exterminated, lock, stock and barrel. . . ." daSilva flicked his eyes, looking in and out, far away and all around. . . . "But who great and meek enough to perform this parable of kindness and fulfilment upon us and to take the condemned bait for ever out of our mouths? Is just there – in the universal frailty of all of us (we is no better than human ants after all, whether we be leader or led) – that the patient trial and duty of ourself really begin. . . ."

"The trial of myself," Stevenson was startled by the prospect of emotional torrents he wished at all costs to avoid. "I thought I had escaped all that. . . ."

"No," daSilva cried sadly. "No virtue for a person in escaping that. You escape not the true trial but the chance to do greater wrongs to the conception of yourself, that's at all. . . I know from me own experience. Trust an evil pork-knocker to tell you the truth. . ." he half-smiled and chuckled.

"Greater wrong to myself. . . ."

"Yes, what's the use of doing more and more injustice to yourself and to everybody who misconceive you as you misconceive them?" DaSilva was a little impatient now. "Don't frighten any more —" he drew upon a storehouse of optimism it had taken him ages to confirm – "I going to tell you a little secret. Is all the unreflective and wrong-headed publication of misfortune in the world you get away from. But that don't mean you dead to the real trial of you, the process of relations in you. . . . To that there may be no end. . . ."

"What the devil are you driving at. . . ?" Stevenson was even more startled.

"The truth is. . ." daSilva rattled on – "a part of you got to linger on indefinitely to gnaw away at the doomsday fastness of things you help to build."

"I suppose you're one of these endless gnawing creatures. . . ." Stevenson could not help sneering a little at the uninhibited speech of this fanatic of the jungle, who sought to express in an hour months of brooding silence, and in a single unbridled day centuries of an instinct for humility and wisdom.

"I believe I am. You are too, Mr. Stevenson. No offence meant." DaSilva spoke without rancour and with the grotesque seriousness which seemed so native to him it gave him the comic and yet serious appearance of laughing at, and killing, the vulgar affliction as well as the isolation of Stevenson and himself. "Call me unfortunate if you like but I live to recall the tale of murder when my captain and crew, engine and boat vanish. I scramble to myself in a cave beside the dead trunk of a man, Cameron, poor Cammy."

He simulated a stab, a groan and a laugh. "Donne,

Jennings as well as me brother – the other daSilva – Vigilance and the rest all disappear." DaSilva pondered on the body of legendary names which were becoming, like his, their own shadowy essence at last.

"Why didn't you disappear with them?"

"How could I go with the hook of a carcass on my conscience? Is I who was left with the thought of Cammy whom people say, erroneously I believe, the other daSilva, my own brother, stab to death. . . ."

"Your brother?" Stevenson was astonished. "Why was he accused of killing the man? Who really did kill him then?"

DaSilva gave Stevenson another sad penetrating look. "Don't worry too much about that." He tried to speak flippantly because flippancy alone would reflect the unself-pitying scales on the underbelly of sentiment. "Who wants to fish, anyway – unless you're caught like me – for murderer or suicide? Believe me. Is a mystery. All injustice is." He sighed. "But sometimes, as I said, you left with no alternative. That's when everybody's death belong to everybody's life like Bible and encyclopedia. So instead of disappearing with my companions I was condemn to remain back, just out of reach of Devil's Hole rapids like if I was jury and judge over myself all rolled in one. . . ." The accursed yet whimsical sentence of guilt and extermination daSilva had affirmed so glibly, even professionally, drew him up, nevertheless, Stevenson knew, from dwelling in even lower quixotic dregs of horror, personal recollection and abysmal surrender to the insecure totality of events. They were both grateful to have been saved, slight as the advantage now appeared, from a greater fall into functional cliché and irresponsibility, wherein they would otherwise have been, whatever their mask of respectability, hopelessly and collectively immersed. "Is a blessing in a curse pull me up to me personal responsible instinct and. . . ."

"A curse in a blessing all the same." Stevenson finished the sentence with a note of rough finality. He was trying once again to thrust aside the motive within the fantastic machinery of relations and conflict which affected him so deeply, but daSilva appeared indifferent to the plea and went on with an air of bloodless and still remorseless passion – "I turning into the ghost of a reporter of the *one* court of conscience after all – comprising nobody else but the mystery of me (or you) – in spite of the f— contradiction on every crowded conventional body's lips. DaSilva. DaSilva," he confessed. "Stevenson. Stevenson," he ejaculated, giving Stevenson an ironical, almost unholy, look. "Somebody or other always addressing me as a flesh-and-barebones seducer – full of tricks – and you for the Jekyll-and-Hyde devil in you name. And yet – " he was laughing outright now –"they say this is the red and blue blood of oral tradition, the ink of noble spirit. I am half-Portuguese, half-Amerindian. As far back in the brutal past as that. And the story of the end of this long phase I still inflicting and suffering, mixing and circulating still but beginning to lose the barbarous depth of its sting. . ." daSilva was laughing at the patched negative scarecrow of himself (pork-knockers were famous for their outlandish self-education and ribald and religious humour) – laughing in earnest as well at every body of tradition the others may have associated with him, and executed him for, in order to feed their own soul with an indignant excuse for hanging on endlessly to the march of innocent conviction and life.

Stevenson lay back and dozed in his hammock conscious of the murmur of the waterfall persisting in the forest like the changing traffic of routine functions and gears of anonymity he had been elected, he dreamed, and paid, as well, to dispense with and still watch. It was a strange embryonic confusing dream to entertain wherein his situation grew into one of profound emergency, detachment and helplessness and therefore inability to rid himself – even while experiencing the freedom of blank repose – from a seeping awareness akin to a marriage of responsibility and contemplation; he found himself half-sinking back into guilty sleep when he woke, and half-rising into broad innocent wakefulness when he slept. He was grateful for the opportunity or privilege – in spite of every contrary emotion – to recline, however uneasily, in the shadow of the noonday sun one step and more above the sounding impulses of flight. He thought he sprang to his feet (but in fact he was sound asleep). DaSilva's smothered voice addressed him from the riverside, announcing his return from the depot at Upper Kamaria where he had gone to collect his boxes of ration.

Stevenson slept. It was not daSilva who had returned. A breeze was stirring in the forest and a whispering tongue of water made a hoarse succulent sound against the river bank. A boat was being grounded or taken out. Stevenson stirred (but felt unable to rouse himself): he recalled the outboard engine he had been inspecting shortly before he lay down and which he had forgotten to restore to its case. It was gross carelessness on his part. Who could tell whether anyone – an enterprising thief perhaps – was round and about?

The dark impression of someone walking across the clearing possessed enduring and anxious substance now but Stevenson felt it would vanish when he looked upon the sun. Yet – he questioned himself closely – where indeed did the real world of perception and apprehension lie? The blind sun was standing high in the sky at this very moment waiting to cross the boundary of every closed eyelid, since this was the frontier of existence supporting the sleeping watcher in feeling or in dismantling the vision of feeling that he, too, was being studied and watched. . . .

DaSilva may have, inadvertently, untied – in releasing his own small craft – the line which secured Stevenson's dinghy. If not daSilva – whose hand then? And the breeze blowing across the forest awoke the slumbering margins of the river until corrugations began to furrow a tranquil brow of cloud joined in reflection to the foot of the land. Stevenson's boat rocked, sensing the possibility of extended movement and edged its way toward the sweep of the current. It heaved and dragged its loose line like a creature moving incautiously backwards with the hook it most feared exercising the walls of its mouth.

A shadow fell on the jungle and on the river, and when the sun emerged the dinghy had been kicked much further away from the landing. The line attached to the bow appeared to stiffen its hold, reluctantly giving way in the end to the pull of the frame as an arm of spray mounted and descended, sprinkling the passage of a minute spider crawling in the hammock of the vessel's interior: it grew difficult to tell where the veined grassroot of one's life commenced and the rocking cliff of illusion ended as the world half-turned on its side eclipsing the native eye of the spider trained on the circumstance of space.

A swallow darted from loops of air and flew straight to the boat to alight on the stern. It flew nervously off as the dinghy, which was running backside foremost, struck a rock. The vessel bounced off and this time when the swallow returned, it chose to fall back upon the bow. The animalcule gaze of the bird crossed the web the spider had spun, as though the frailest refraction of vision occurred, swift as a glistening bead of water on dispersing and immaterial fabric. It was a fleeting coincidence established out of spiralling visionary moments; in the spider's terrestrial universe the sky was precariously revolving around the earth, a sky whose silken broken texture one could conceivably have built; in the swallow's flying instinct the earth was leaning upwards condensed out of every shattered cobweb which held a running stream together like an instinctual ball one could never – in one's wildest imagination – have invented or made. . . .

4

Stevenson stirred. A voice was ringing in his ears and the drowned choir of the waterfall echoed across the forest. He was so convinced he had heard someone that he was surprised there was no one without. He could scarcely believe his eyes when he looked around again and saw the dinghy was no longer harnessed to the landing. It had vanished. He recalled confusedly (as one does after the involuntary reins of sleep in the hot race of the day) the exaggerated sensation he had experienced, half-daydream, half-nightmare, of the wrecked boat. The galvanic flood of recollection ebbed across the broad painted clearing of daylight into the black brush of forest and river in the way monstrous fears and inflated loves are inclined to shrink and retire into pools of aridity after bearing the headlong nervous orchestration of the senses.

Ten chances to one the dinghy was standing unspectacularly against an arm of rock. . . . And if it had actually succeeded in running the gauntlet (a difficult feat without guidance or assistance from anyone) daSilva would undoubtedly have secured it when it came within view of the depot at Upper Kamaria.

There was always, of course, the devil's chance to be reckoned with, that it had galloped through another channel, driven by wind and current until it drew close to the inevitable brink of the falls where the frightful pace of the current turned taut and smooth as a memorial tablet. Here indeed there was no alternative but to sink into the grave-yard of hope. . . .

Stevenson felt a little sick – empty of speculation and thwarted by desire. It was extraordinary what uncharted poles arose out of the jungle which forced one to venture into an interior where one saw oneself turned inside out. It was fear, the ceaseless fear of entering this state of internal and external abandonment which epitomized the mystery of the bush.

It was the selfish fear of experiencing fear, the selfish love of the possession of love one was being summoned to transcend or see through by abiding to a steadfast covenant and refusal to shrink from the extremity and volume of the demoralizing contact and content of death.

The fear of every strange outpost of the mind, every strange planet within the ambivalent orbit of self-discovery, became concrete in the jungle since it involved a corre-sponding station where the spirit of the seasons was single and changeless, the summer of the sun was continuous and universal, the affluence of the stars never varied, and only the river of space rose and declined, drowning one's solitary outpost or stripping one down to the nakedness of reality. Every vestige of a man-made environment, the former accumulation of longing and excess, trapped in the past, was reduced to a grandiose whim of nature. One sought, nev-ertheless, greedily and vicariously, to embrace this over and over again as frequently and intimately as the tides of memory would allow, even if this renaissance of the images of desire led to a fresh contamination of the soul of a new universe. One saw, in this old recurring emotional gauge of fact, the genuine human impossibility of *breaking through* beyond oneself, and this recognition of the limitations of the muse evoked the greatest fear of all, the fear that every elaborate means, however varied and admirable in encompassing distances in space, always accomplished the same end in time. . . . That end was either bound to be immanent and greater than oneself (in which case it implied the immaterial acceptance of an open and eternal creation and fulfilment), or forever conceivable and restricted and final and incapable of true realization in any span of accomplishment. . . .

Having said all this he felt like a man who had ridden across the selfsame area of choices dozens of times. Except that now – for the first essential poverty-stricken time in his life – all the richness and variety of the earth had been reduced to a single letter of fortune in which he had banked all his past energies and resources. This was his last letter to his mistress, Maria, and in a moment of self-contempt and fear and desire for her still he had flung it into the bottom of the dinghy to rot in the sun and rain. Needless to say he would have rescued it in an emergency but now it might be too late.

And yet might it not be a blessing in disguise if he were compelled – out of the emergent lateness of the hour – *compelled* (Stevenson was fascinated by the thought of such simplicity to destiny) to dispense with restoring the machinery of love (his mind grieved like a child – though he would have been too proud to admit it to anyone but himself – and wandered over a wide field of failed duties and associations) – to dispense with the wooden fragments of emotional disaster which he used to dwell in, and still sought to animate, largely for reasons of inspired horror or self-gratification?

Bear in mind (Stevenson was listening to the absurd – because shatteringly impartial – voice of consciousness), every restoration of dead loves and glories invited him to experience again – and this was bound to be the most cruel trial of all – the acute climax of reality whose timely explosion had been intended to compensate him for those factors of recurring deficit he used to possess, the debt he owed eternity, the realization no man escapes, of material incapacity, which comes as certainly and inevitably as death.

Would it not be wisdom, the true wisdom of the soul, to see every fragment of his world – the last sodden letter to his mistress – as an invaluable morsel, in its broken right, offered to the naked person in the heart of one's guilt and hunger for recreation? Who it was that fed one (the anonymous midwife and middleman of the ages) and who the person one helped, in turn, to feed, possessed an answer equally in the spirit of the jungle as in the spectre of dismantling a rose.

Was this devouring plea the ultimate letter he had been driven to write to Maria and then tossed away from him into the rapids because he felt so ashamed and exposed?

Stevenson awoke the next morning with the lucid feeling of not having slept a wink. His staring lucidity lay in this acute, if grotesque, confrontation with a larger symbolic awareness of himself transcending the crippled sleep of existence – reminding him of how the dead may recall the royal substance of the living and an amputated trunk still dream of suffering uncommon pangs with every exertion of a phantom limb. Such unnatural lucidity was also an involuntary conviction that enslavement to archetypal models of insensibility was a glaring illusion the temperament of freedom endures in the revolting and self-conscious apparatus of time. . . .

DaSilva had not yet returned and Stevenson decided to set out for the Upper Kamaria depot – a matter of two miles or so – by a pork-knocker's dying trail he understood to run the entire way along the bank. He pinned a large sheet of paper upon the rail of the steps and scrawled – in capital letters – the hasty anxious note:

SHALL TRY TO FOLLOW ANCIENT LINE TO DEPOT. HOPE TO MAKE IT AND BACK BY NOON. DINGHY GONE FROM LANDING.

He gave his leg a rueful thump. . . . He had actually stumbled upon a surreptitious arm of the trail creeping down to the clearing, a week or two ago, and he picked it up again now skirting the side of a hill. He began to exercise his prospecting knife, judiciously lopping, every now and then, a finger – or the skin of the elbow – from a branch, in order to define afresh every step he made.

The direction he followed was inclined to turn one with the body of the bush like a study of a primitive ordeal of initiation which involved keeping an eye on every aspect of the anatomy of place not to lose the way. Each old guiding incision, old as the decay of centuries after a month or two, was hardening into the arteries of the bush. It was a miracle a fluid passage still remained. And all at once Stevenson sensed with a start he was coming into a relatively clearer opening which began to clothe him with the impression he was leaving a congested corridor and entering the skin of a new communication, even community, light-hearted, trimmed, in fact so recently groomed each severed leaf or limb was freshly and gaily tinted with its own transparent juice or blood.

Someone had recently passed and worked a random vein in the line. Stevenson felt the cutting sensation of a presence so near him it lifted his heart like fruit into his mouth. He began, to tremble, not with alarm but with the thrill of nervous signals and noises, his own loud indigestible breathing, the tingle of arrows of perspiration in the roots of his hair, the rustle of his clothing like the clatter of impossible sticks of armour in a gale, the intimate forest of relations like an army on the march branching to enlist him after their aeons of stubborn withdrawal from human contact.

He responded, with another thrill of recognition, to the deep seductive strategic pull of nature and history mingling together like a unique revelation which, in overwhelming, would beach him upon that middle jigsaw distance of sacrificial personality which lies between the individual darkness of temperament and the universal blind logic of material suns. He felt the willing trespassing footfall of the forest, the voice of the waterfall upon a distant breeze, and looking up – far above – he tried to pierce the vast umbrella of leaves where the dark sun glittered and broke into the minute fall of stars through texture like drawn fabric.

The air of the bush swam with thin vapour like idealized smoke rising from the buried fires of the underworld. There was no saying where he stood – relatively virgin territory or some ancient buried wistful encampment. All around were stately greenheart trees, mature and stalwart. He knew them by the cracked silvery etchings on the bark of their trunk wherein they confessed both age and humility. They had been successful in maintaining their rooted stand against the inventive forces which sought to lay hold of them. Time and time again companies had endeavoured to make use of the rich stocks of timber they represented.

But the difficulty in transportation was enormous. It was useless taking them through crowded and forbidden rapids and it became necessary to draw them along rude trails overland, around the falls, to the nearest suitable point downriver where it would be safe to float them on rafts. The expense involved cancelled the hope of every farthing of profit.

Stevenson liked to muse on the company he served as an enterprising group of new pioneer woodcutters and businessmen who would build a solid road in the future which would eventually begin to pay for itself. Furthermore, he dreamt, such a road would stand upon the involuntary spiritual accumulations of the past, the paradoxical personal failures of time (his gamble was one such slender trial of identity, stretched to the limits of fearful endurance) which reconciled the alien defensive march of the jungle to yield to the timeless intruder and enlist into its ranks, for the first true time, the patient long-suffering forces in the heart and continuous depth of reason. It was touch-and-go like fish to bait, flame to match, the essential inner and outer realities of construction, life-in-death, death-in-life, in all of which one learnt how to convert oneself in and beyond the life of leviathan, half-machine, half-human surviving instincts, the natural misconceptions of the created body of all creatures and man.

Stevenson suddenly recalled a vision of Kaiser hunting for meat in the heart of the forest, calling to the creatures of the bush by blowing his breath against the edge of a dry leaf; he (Stevenson) felt the selfsame lust and sap rise within him now to test the sensual spirit of collaboration. He chose a fading leaf which had turned stiff as paper and blew a crisp note. A whirling shape of sound arose, thin as the outline of a letter and frail as a cry – devoid of tears or sentiment it was so aerial and still profound – of an animal calling to its mate. The sigh of the trees joined his whistling breath and extended his plea into the distance, giving it a mere hint of whispering passion, no more, like the plaintive bottomless air of a poem. *If only she would answer,* Stevenson thought, forgetting himself as he blew, *Maria! the runaway heart of love one had to hunt down like a wayward beast.* The subtle organ of the leaf cracked like the ghost of a whip and the grating dying sound awoke him to the reality of the rustle of dry living feet. Stevenson grew cold, stock-still, waiting and listening. Something or someone jumped into the trail at his feet. *There she was.* The cry of the leaf had borne fruit. It was a brown creature like a rabbit with the soft eyes of a fable of the forest. They both became numb with surprise; the hallucinated blood of both hunter and hunted rose and darkened their eyes. He tightened his grip on the prospecting knife he carried and a thread of hesitation upheld and restrained his arm, binding – in the same trick of light – the feminine creature which had not yet sensed the vital presence of danger. He realized he must act now or lose her forever. The energy and passion of the chase pulled him down to her even as the twine of vision, which chained her to him, held his heart and body upright and steady. An enormity of symbolic frustrated desire clamoured bitterly, urging him to cut and strike; and the shrewd compliant voice of necessity addressed him, reducing everything to a game of nothing – here was fresh meat for his pot. . . . It was a tableau of subjective feeling, combining far-flung motive as well as helpless substitute and image, the involuntary daring suspension of cruelty in the grotesque heart of love; the knife remained poised like a sword without falling and the soft brown eyes opened to the full light of peril and darted like a streak into the bush.

When he emerged at Upper Kamaria, an hour after setting out from his own station, Stevenson was relieved to find daSilva's boat tied to the landing. The door of the depot was open and a note had been stuck outside upon a protruding nail. Stevenson did not see this until he entered the depot and came back outside again.

Inside he had found Kaiser's ledger sprawled open and a leaf ripped from the middle. There was a bottle of ink and the nib of the pen lying beside it showed fresh clotted traces of use.

Outside, on the door, the letters inscribed on the remnant torn from the ledger were beginning to run into a duel of elongated fingers and decimated characters after a nightfall of dew. And – even before that – they bore the print of daSilva's hand as if the latter had been intent on openly concealing what he wrote.

Stevenson scanned the intimate wounds and shadows running into each other across the broken page and discerned what appeared to be an abrupt communiqué addressed to friend or enemy:

SOMEBODY STEAL MY RATIONS.

WHO?

GONE TO TELL KAISER.

That was all but it left him with the taste of conspiracy and shock. Who – in God's name – had spied upon the depot when Kaiser and he were there and stolen poor daSilva's rations? And – another thing – were daSilva and Kaiser allowing themselves to grow into the dupes of someone or something they both knew? He had scarcely asked himself the question when he was conscious of a sharp gruesome feeling of exposure under the cruel sword of the sun. He wondered if, in coming bareheaded into the open out of the bush, he had suffered a mild attack of sunstroke. The hypochondriac misgiving drew him to turn, almost with a gentle desire for succour, to the blunted cover of light in the jungle. . . . What a shocking reversal of temperament this was in a man who worshipped the sun. He was beginning to look into the obscurity he had once turned away from as if he now knew, instinctively, perhaps, like a stricken sensitive relation of the animal kingdom, that every climate of terror and essential clearing of security were actually the same umbrella, capable of providing spiritual cover or becoming equally just another naked inhospitable material pole.

The road around the Kamaria rapids possessed no conspicuous signals for Stevenson when he set out to look for Kaiser and daSilva. His eyes, however, were beginning to grow sharper than a needle. The road was located to exploit ridges of land, powerful subsidiary watersheds shooting to the rapids; and all at once they began to fall away naturally from him – to lose their overwhelming contour – and in the process his emotions fell into step within him upon a meaningful thread of being. In this way he was able to offset – by reason of such a promissory highway – the extraordinary dense machine and labyrinth of the jungle: the rude portage he followed was sliding into a genuine ribbon of sensibility along which and over which breathed the essential vapour of personality. If indeed this emanation was a guide leading to the spectre of place he was beginning to glimpse, or to the creation of the watch he was beginning to read – if indeed it was all these, then this was a natural true gift he possessed after all, the evocation of visible proportions, however delicate. And such proportions turned the frailest outline in space into the lineaments of the quarry of the muse, something larger than pure spirit. Something which provided a signal of love as well as of danger – the inflation of every conscious ravine which yawned next to the road under his feet. . . . He was now approaching a hairpin bend just beyond which the land appeared to fall precipitously. Smooth trunks of trees came close to the brink on either side of the chasm, extending the singular fan of their branches so that the foliage became a knitted curtain through which holes still existed upon a rectangular skylight which divided the architecture of the forest. Beneath this it was plainly different. All concealment was lacking of an open cleavage in the floor or carpet of the forest like a giant's coffin, forty feet wide, the vertical sides of which – in the shock of construction – were beset by many boulders.

The bend in the roadway was scarcely more than twelve feet from the edge of the chasm and he was addressed by an urgent pleading voice. A chattering broke out overhead and a monkey could be discerned signalling and wiping his comic sad eyes in the bush. Stevenson made his way to the very brink of the land where a sprinkling of creatures crossed and recrossed the curtain over the void. They were involved, he realized, in a kind of elaborate subterfuge in the air above him as they cavorted their tails like roots of mysterious substitution for apprehensive humanity, the gods whose joy and sorrow they aspired to bind and relate. . . . His eyes slid along the curtain with them and were drawn down at last as if they were antennae of foreboding slowly inclining to cling to the depths of the ravine. He understood at last – with terrifying clarity – what the mimics of his fate were declaring. Lodged within two boulders – in a grotesque upright position on the opposite wall beneath him – was the body of a man.

The legs appeared fragile and unbroken, one arm easily pinned, the other outflung in a strange dancing movement. The figure and face looked like that of a stranger. . . . Stevenson stared. Was it Kaiser? Was it daSilva? Who was it? The vacillating smoke issuing from the ravine began to lift, and the antics of the living and dead – animal parody and statuesque deliberation – grew wholly into his consciousness of them. He craned his neck forward staring. . . and staring, suspended between dreadful compassion and curiosity, half-monkey, half-man. . . . *It was daSilva after all who stood stark and dead though so changed in twenty-four hours he could have been Kaiser or Cameron or Stevenson himself.* And if he appeared to be now aping and declaring the fiery hellish metamorphosis in the body of other men's dying, they had long been involved in deciphering the living riddle of his ancient conquest of men. In fact the gamble of the extinction of empire in his illegible features – compounded of the sovereign of death as well as the servant of life – was capable of germinating the conscience of time, the new word of being, and filling each native body of physical measurement and rule with the bait of science or individual legend, the enormity of personal conception and shared misconception.

BOOK THREE

CREATION OF THE WATCH

These metaphors are more than mere metaphors, they are borrowed from the realm of reality. . . non-spectacular reality.

GABRIEL MARCEL
The Mystery of Being

Look, as if we were alone on the earth, lost between dream and life, look at that mysterious flower. . . . See the inconsolable rose.

VILLIERS DE L'ISLE-ADAM
Axël
(trans. by J. P. Seward)

5

Kaiser's house at Lower Kamaria had been built in sight of the foot of the rapids where it kicked the river for the last dreaming time before settling into a stabler body of water which now ran into navigable harness to the Atlantic coast. Each iridescent bubble bore the painted carriage of sky and trees like an exquisite moment of reflection seeming to confirm and fulfil in its own shell volumes of pouring water. It was in pursuit of such a fragile symbol in nature, illuminating the identity of the restless capture of resources, that both daSilva and Stevenson had set out from Upper Kamaria to consult Kaiser. The bubble of time they sought was sweeping past the landing at Kaiser's house even then (the moment each one chose to set out) carrying a portrait of place broken down to an ant's eye view of the passing world. Nevertheless the substance of detail was clear, shining with the brilliance of the star of the sun.

The ancient house was deserted, the crumbling garage padlocked, and one was just able to discern – by peering through a crack in the bubbling sun on the window – the face of a clock on the opposite wall. The clock had stopped at two minutes to four early in the morning or, who could tell, it may have been earlier still, yesterday in the afternoon, a couple of hours after Kaiser had left Kamaria for Bartica. He had left a sign on the door – CLOSED, GONE TO COLLECT SUPPLIES – and one knew from this that the caretaker was away on one of his lightning trips. . . . It was nearer to ten than four. The clock within the cottaged bubble had stopped no one knew when.

Buoyed up like a stone floating phenomenally on a pool it resisted falling and spending logical ring after ring to enlarge the area it shattered. Supported and insulated as it now was between the death of morning and the birth of afternoon, between individual darkness and light, it existed – like a treaty superior to the temperament of wars in the past – to recreate forever its own lucid middle distance and womb, transposing the centre of universal reflection to the circumference and realizing a new centre of need upon each new circumference. . . .

The image of the empirical caretaker's house, burnt black as the husbandman of the sun and reduced and still curiously distended within the transparency of time, was silently addressed by a looming face and arrival. A woman had come abruptly out of the bush, Amerindian, midnight hair on her shoulders, so jet-black it looked as if her headdress was one perpetual plait and stroke of mourning. Her eyes were sad, blacker than numerals of ink and yet devoid of the sinister humour of self-pity. It was a feature of unsentimentality she had inherited from her mother's tribe in the Brazilian/Guianan heartland. But this near-stoic uncomplaining predisposition had been refined by a legacy of individual temperament, stemming from her father's side, Portuguese or Spanish, which made it possible for her to maintain, in the heart of violent circumstance – the death of a husband, father or son – the ceremony of participating in their end with dignity.

She possessed for these and other reasons the propriety and impropriety of the muse of the jungle – the heart as well as the heartlessness of the new world – and it would have been ludicrous, if not narrow and pretentious, to call her an ordinary evildoer or thief. It was true the old prospecting bag on her shoulders was capable of disgorging daSilva's stolen rations as well as other curious odds and ends. But then there was also an imposing fullness to her figure; she was far gone with child. She put her sack down and reclined against the wall of Kaiser's house contemplating the bush downriver within which she had carefully hidden an Indian corial. Her every movement and glance were filled with a cruel deliberation like a study in guarding an inner repose. She felt it would be unwise to set out before nightfall in case she ran into Kaiser in his outboard-driven craft on the rivertop – on his way back to his station – and he stopped and questioned her about her belongings as he had the right to do.

The woman was now leaning the tired animal frame of her back (or so it seemed to her in a sudden fever of exhaustion) against the distended wall of the house as she reflected how long it would be for the first cool pinpoint star of darkness to flare.... The streaming glare was becoming too much for her and she was grateful for every moment of eclipse. Each time she closed her eyes she moved the ball of the sun from another burning intolerable ray to the dark captive pole of time. The fact was (and this was the peculiar lesson she was beginning to learn) she could no longer resist the soul of human fatigue which – in overwhelming and overshadowing her – gave her a new and frail light of adjustment in relation to every dense journey she had made out of the far savannah of the sun. This new match-stick of dream gave her the promised support of reason like the secret leg of flight she needed still to make, from hunted or hunting station to each threatened depot – across centuries it seemed of scorched self-surrender and self-arrival – until her limbs, animal-wise still, became the personal meas-ure of extinction and flame to offset a holocaust of birth and death.

Every strange, even tortured, mask of civilization she had acquired along the way from brutal tribe to the dreaming constellation of humanity, from animal servitude to bearing the burden of the world's need for love – all these seemed to grow inwards into the unsentimental chorus which is related to the epic origins of the mother of the brood. The dark voice of the river at her feet hissed like the stitch of stars upon every flowing button of her attire which was ripping loose. One outstretched hand had begun to tear a loud seam under her arm and down the running side of her dress, while the other still appeared to lie against her like the silent lock in a door sealed upon the brow of abdomen. . . . The unravelling stitch of lightning-travail and pain darted more fiercely still into her sleeping mind, with the fragility and yet searing force of an electric alphabet of nerves, making her almost visually aware of a pulse within a pulse, a heartbeat so much more immensely frail than her own. She shuddered, clutching at the sack of herself and fearing both thunderclap and subtle theft of the universal organ she carried within.

The outline of pain subsided, leaving her with a message of an open and steep frame in the mind, an abrupt escarpment towards which Stevenson and Kaiser were even now moving, on the floor of the river beneath her as well as along one high ridge or leg above, but never – in her fiercely-repressed anxiety – actually arriving in time to help her. It was as if the desperate banqueting table of history and the table of a law were turned on its side and she became the faint one, now leaning upon it, who needed guests and attention. In the wild strong past it had been different. It had been daSilva and his companions who stood in need of her and pursued the tribe to which she belonged, wooing her and compelling her to come out of the wilderness to succour the life of Donne and his crew before they perished with their backs to the wall.

The fact was that Stevenson had moved even closer than she knew into intimate correspondence with her and reconstruction of it all, so that he was in a position to observe daSilva as if he saw through him into her mounting agony, across the gulf which still yawned at his feet. Kaiser, too, even now might be able to assist her if she struggled up and descended into the bowl of the river to establish beyond the last flicker of doubt that the banquet of reality they shared, life-in-death, death-in-life, was now finished and indivisible. But she felt herself symbolically pinned to the caretaker's house as daSilva was supported within the order of place and both had become the host of a besieged mankind, needing to draw into each other new flesh and blood from the helpful herd and pack. It was a spiritual invitation of need turning into the enduring life and greed of the muse – incorporating conqueror and conquered, hunter and hunted – towards which all men, because of the cleavage in their natures, forever inclined as to their saddest and noblest elevation. . . .

When it was discovered by the tribe amongst whom she had returned – full of murder and hate – that she was with child for Donne, the Captain of the boat (others pointed their finger at daSilva), they had sent her away again, out of the savannahs into which they had fled – not back to Donne's estate, but to Kartabo Point, a small settlement facing Arian Island. This gateway in the middle of the river looked towards the asylum of Kartabo and back again towards the foot of the Kamaria falls. And there was often a longing air – the curbed and delicate air of spring – around Kartabo, which Arian Island was able to sustain by sluicing and checking the current, and disseminating it as through a sieve until seeds of spray were all that remained, to remind one of one's immunity from the falls. On the other hand the hint of a new freshness in the wind spoke of the far Atlantic breezes. . . . It was at Kartabo Point that one found the beginnings of a new legendary continental offspring born of many races.

Here also grew the changing sky of rumour as though a cloudy existence sought occasionally to conceal men from the image of themselves and to constitute a seasonal fastness like a variable depot of faculties bordering on the erosive and equally accretive substance of ancient feud and abandon, address and command. Whatever alien principle of cohesion they were now individually capable of choosing (and embodying with stoical and native self-determination) sprang out of each subjective act of terrifying submission to the summons of agents whose names betokened obedience to a sovereign recluse.

And this seal had become the compulsive goal of love and authority standing naturally within each royal person, who grew, because of such grand responsible proportions, to live in need of humility and the labour of others. . . . It was the most dangerous and jealous profession in the world, the prosecution of human loyalties and affairs, the approach to an amalgam of allegiance, animal and spiritual, one began for the first glimmering time of rare distinction and flitting being and experience, to carry wholly within oneself. . . .

It was difficult to tell when the ring had commenced to close around daSilva. Perhaps it had started at the very outset when he and Petra (she had given herself this new name, Amerindians were famous for adopting a diversity of titles) were struggling across a faint landscape, in the dreamlike company of ghostly pursuers. A faint landscape it was because of the eclipse of time, the end of a long hazardous phase of discovery and conquest, an eclipse which allowed a light otherwise too reticent for brightness to illumine the pilot of the mind. This faintness was akin to a constellation of renewal and rebirth appearing, for this age and time, in the underworld sky of the jungle, and upon a horizon which coincided with the end of empires when the darkness of rule becomes the absolute light of consciousness. Such involuntary associations – subtler than conventional upbringing and station would allow – were real for the woman she was: real in the way every symbolic jungle becomes to those who are steeped in the intimate species of its inhabitants until the vision of what is buried and alive suddenly transcends a fixed limb or region of historical value. All of this signified she was now in painful contact with a pressing wellnigh clamouring burden of existence. . . .

The absurd question which still haunted her mind was this: on her expulsion from the savannahs had she actually succeeded in making the long journey downriver past Arian Island to the asylum at Kartabo? Or was it that, having arrived there, she returned to Kamaria, on the full tide of pregnancy, in response to a drifting letter which told how her ancient tribe were closing around daSilva to kill him? She shuddered violently against the raft of Kaiser's house. Had she paddled this way to try and warn him or to join the others in overpowering him? It seemed to her exciting and extraordinary that the ultimatum of feud could have struck in association with someone like herself whose origins were so defaced in the currency of the tribe.

It was true that they had long succeeded in repressing the fact of her mixed racial stock and had had no qualms about protecting her when she returned to them, pursued by the ghosts of Donne and his crew. Had the slumbering desire for war awakened when they later discovered she was with child, no one knew for certain for whom? Was it the fact of ambiguous parentage – once more asserting itself to their displeasure – which excited an instinct for rage? Was it a long-forgotten access of pride harbouring degradation and misery? Or was it a debt they needed to repay, half-gift, half-theft? Whatever solemn incongruous reason there was, it might equally be a carnival clue to the past when the snake of the tribe sought to shed its skin and to slay the conception (or misconception) of the self. But this purity of savage distinction was becoming ridiculous and impossible now in the light of the elusive creature they set upon to kill within the constraint of an enormous tide bringing one face to face with the fragile reflection of oneself in a continuous and indestructible process of arriving everywhere and nowhere. The collision of the fictions of past and future grew into the selfsame stroke of identity, place and circumstance. . . .

At the time when her expulsion from the body of the tribe occurred, it left her dazed and beaten, immersed in the heart of a painful brooding insensibility, like one beginning to learn to live on technical scraps of stunned memory in a way she had only glimmeringly perceived before in a series of losses, raids and deprivations. It was as if she had no alternative but to venture to invent a soul which would now stand a certain distance away from the ancient feeling for existence. And this shared remove grew into the grafted instinct or muse of self-creation which seemed to drive her away from and yet restore and approach the numinous food of life.

The first steps she made appeared to raise her to a dazed elevation, a new stage upon which she dwelt like one manufactured for a ghost. And yet nothing within her or without succeeded in eclipsing entirely the old tribal mystery and knowledge that she was being followed and watched. It filled her, frail as the intuition was, with the mourning timeless subsistence of dread and compassion. . . . She was crossing the swelling savannahs towards the line of the river and the forest. The secret watchers or guardians she sensed were nowhere in sight and the surface of the ground nearly everywhere looked hard and stony; in some curious way she felt capable of growing attuned to this over and above irrational foreboding or longing. The watch of indifference the landscape turned on her confirmed the link within her of grotesque freedom drawn out of the sensibility of pure bondage which barters the heart of love's slave until it arrives at that moving centre from which it can survey what it has gained and lost in the traffic of liberation. Beardless stone, the most enduring replica of eternal youth, groomed by the elements, lay side by side with unshaven granite, that ageless merchant bearing the shallow flesh of earth out of which the straggling hair of vegetation grew.

On the banks of the meandering streams arose an occasional exotic lampshade of trees, apparently discarded by savage nature and shimmering against a transparent bulb of heat, half-sky, half-burning cloud, like the radiation of glass, or the bland mask a clock wears when it refracts the spider of the sun into the selfsame legs as arms.

Far away on one open hand the mountains were slowly cooking; a signal rose into the air, pensively inclining down to the waving bank of the river in corresponding loops and half-loops. This half-fluid ribbon, letters of smoke, advertising the tenanted or untenanted lodge of the landscape, faded as though to the slow extinction of an invisible fire. In the stark retentive clarity of the sun, the ancient grey-beard of the savannahs seemed abnormally removed from the nightmare green of the neighbouring forest, like the selective plate of genius, on which the buzzing wings of a ferocious fly were photographed in the memory, hovering a full inch from one's forehead, almost inclined not to settle and sting, as if isolated in a jar, within which it was free to pose as both the gaoler and the gaoled since each creature without, upon which it reflected, stood actually within an identical self-reversing bubble. . . .

Moving upon such a still dreamlike plateau and within such a shield of distance Petra longed to relinquish herself to be consumed within sight of the commanding tableland of the mountains. Let the air swarm with flies, the myriad representative flies of the jungle, as of vultures, flies, too, constellated in space, falling from the brooding jigsaw lower depths of heaven. It did not rest with fly, or vulture however, since she felt herself already being devoured alive and driven along by intimate gnawing teeth within, the fiery rodent of the law, running up her thighs to the navel of birth.

Towards afternoon all trace of shadow vanished from the plateau. Petra was fast approaching the brink of the fall, when the sleeping river loses its poise and drops like a smoking breath down the face of the Kaieteuran escarpment; here nature had long established – and history had now slowly begun to read and confirm – both the desolate link and the message of a divided reality, the displacement of man like riverbed from river, watershed and island from the heart of a continent. Across the shadowless uplifted stage of the plateau the breathless features of age and youth acquired the look of unbroken caretaker symbols of the solid food of memory by establishing an original station of departure for every ghostly messenger or thief or usurper of value.

The fluctuating currency which supported the life of every poor depot, place of barter or trade, centre for administering the affairs of grant or estate, had its golden standard and mean in this unbroken ritual quarry – however crushing and illusory it often appeared – enticing one to adventure still beyond areas of settlement and achievement. For this was the faculty of unity which focused one's energy and attention upon an extreme frontier where neither psychological stain nor shadow persisted to block one's efforts to descend to those continually dispossessed of everything with the naked act of being born, or the naked act of dying to the creative memory of themselves. This was the moment when she became aware of herself as a pregnant ally in the creaturely march of things which vanish into a body of conquest in order to lend support in preserving and still devouring the spirit of the sun. . . .

(In approaching Kaiser's house, where Petra lay in the grotesque extension of travail, Stevenson thought he saw a remote – because at that moment repulsive – resemblance to the mistress of his dreams. . . . It was as if a living boulder had detached itself from the wall of the escarpment where the dead man daSilva was pinned, crushing the vessel, containing the letter Stevenson had written to Maria, into a most alarming and brutal and vivid signature or exposure beyond idle recrimination or love. . . . What habit of address could he still muster in such gratuitous conversion and extremity, flesh become stone, and stone the alphabet of blood?

The fact was – Stevenson sought to control his emotion – here was a strong and primitive woman, with the strength of rock and of naked eloquence and element only the truly inarticulate possess because they are capable of invoking the image of every man's conception and misconception of misfortune. . . . Thus it was – like a numinous boulder informed by legs and arms as well as by the universal heart of man – Petra struggled to rise and resume the journey of the past which had begun the very day she crossed the everlasting plateau

mesmerized by her own plight, abandonment and weakness which
seemed – in spite of everything – to endure into a distinct and free
motive to incorporate the flight of time and draw assistance out of
granite. . . .)

6

Towards afternoon the air seemed to swarm with the frailest
character of dust; this was the aspect which had momentarily
killed all shadow on the Kaieteuran plateau. It was one the
clouds occasionally assumed over the Guiana highlands, an
extraordinary denigration of atmosphere wherein the elements appeared conspiring to compute that the wind of a
forgotten desert still blew over the massive shelf of the savannahs
and upon the dense climate of the rain forest. Why did this
jigsaw of fertility consist in consuming itself within a sunless
proliferation, while marrying the barren memories of earth
and sun into a realm of equal seed or potency as dust? This was
the controversial question of subsistence – in the significant
consciousness of every dreamer – wasteland or heartland.

On her coming nearer to the escarpment and the roar of the
fall, the small floating dust actually touched her skin for the
first time, an almost imperceptible spray which barely mois-
tened her fingers when she drew them along wrist and arm.
This settlement and film were rare in the light of the heavy
drenching rainfall that often fell in the region, and in fact the
sprinkling sensation she felt was neither conventional rain nor
dust: it had come drifting over the face of the plateau, after
rising from the waterfall, upwards and along like the smoothest
intangible petals of a rose which were neither skin nor dew. . . .
And now for the first time the sharp bitter, almost agonizing
odour of the jungle, like a knife in a fibrous stamen of rotting
meat, one grew to take for granted, came to her throat and

nostrils. The savannahs were becoming more heavily populated with presences of trees which began to merge into the gathering at the fringe of the forest.

The shadowy gate of being which had appeared in an instant to close like a veil over the plateau was present once again upon the ground, punctuating the falling leaves of mist with open bars or marks and wounded stops or discolourations. These hinges of ultimatum – the imperfect frame as well as the trunk and scent of danger or disaster, the grotesque feeling that she was being followed and watched before being stroked and smitten and flung to her death down the wall of the cliff – still drove her on to the deadly goal of the escarpment where the nervous ladder of the trail led to the river beneath. She was being inescapably drawn forward, as well as pushed from behind, by a community of unfulfilled emotion whose identity – brutal as stone, uncertain as water, immaterial as breath – was an expression of compulsive command and dangerous summons she could not evade. The fortress of the past was yielding to a timeless rent and sacrifice in the mother of the present, a design native to all conquest of place in the past, present and future, and there was no prospect of turning back for anyone, pursuers or pursued, since to step back was to find a suspended gate leading and pointing again into the heart of the future. . . .

(On approaching the nightmare bend in the Kamaria portage, da Silva felt a heavy blow glance along the back of his head and strike him upon his shoulders. The misty coffin and escarpment which awaited him constituted a universal recurring fault in a landscape both he and Petra knew by heart – as if they were actually involved with all mankind in sharing the same dream of death and eating the involuntary substance of place within each timeless hungry moment. . . . DaSilva groaned with gratification, rather than protest and surprise, under the force of the blow. The fact was he lived in constant expectation of being attacked in this sudden riddling way, though he was often deceived by the spirit of anti-climax which dwelt in the bush, and which

appeared to draw him back time and time again from dramatic overburden and extinction in the meaningless wealth of the jungle's appetite. Was it possible that now at last he would be able to turn, half-stunned by the blow he had been given, and see the fulfilled thing or being, the fellowship of loved or hated one, woman or man, muse or monster, which had long haunted him, and which he had come to desire and dread, in the way one dreads the actuality while inspired by the thought of freedom from possession?

This was the complex hunger – so native to the pork-knocker – which he grew to entertain over long years spent living within the claustrophobic springs of nature, in the midst of shocks of continuous deprivation, and in an isolation which robbed him of everything conventionally human save the salvage of unique responses and the thread of personality. . . . *Now* he recovered sufficiently to spin around. . . . No one was there. But he found it hard to believe he had been tricked once again by idle circumstance. If not by this, by whom then, and by what? He was still too dazed to reason properly and to frame another inadequate conviction and reply. A heavy rotting branch had fallen upon him out of the forest. That was all but the blow had possessed a venomous, almost calculating, strength and severity. The bark had split like a matchbox with the expenditure of fire and energy, and a stifling brooding smell rose, like acrid smoke, into his nostrils. It had the effect of rousing him to take fresh stock of himself. . . . He brushed the crumbs of mould and plaster from his back and shoulders on to the ground which was already carpeted with leaves and debris in all stages of vegetation and decomposition.

DaSilva recalled – dazed still by the blow he had been given in his half-famished condition – the dog which had been his companion until the day of its death six months ago. The animal had been a gift from Kaiser who possessed something of an eye for those evil-looking creatures which turned out to be such faithful and good friends in the body of the interior. A thin mongrel beast it was, wearing the air of a frisky spirit, whose resources were swift bone and leather and the laughing snout of an alligator; yet giving the appearance, too, of such curious light immobility and grieving tension, it could have been created out of shavings fastened together with an unkempt steadfastness which seemed untrustworthy, at first sight, and yet so innocuous and lasting it was fascinatingly economic and right.

The poor starving beast had died all of a sudden when daSilva had moved into a hazardous and crushing region, following a vein of gold prospection which was overlaid by transparent droppings in association with a crop of quartz like sheep in brutal clothing flocking the ground, all of which pointed not only to gold but to a deposit of diamonds as well. Nothing materialized quickly enough, however, to make the expedition worth while. The trail continued to lead not only deeper into the forest but into the bowels of the ground and beyond the command of the primitive mining tools at a pork-knocker's disposal. The slender stocks of food began to vanish. The game began to grow more reticent than ever with a dry spell which had invaded the bush. . . . DaSilva was now digging compulsively with his scavenging toe into the present carpet of the Kamaria forest as he visualized the dog Kaiser had given him burrowing in the past into mournful faeces for food. The ghostly reflection of the faithful animal which he stirred into existence with his foot seemed intent as ever before in locating a diseased crumb which had fallen from the bruise in his (daSilva's) back. . . .

The action of the dog possessed a peculiar significance for daSilva who recalled that it coincided with his recovery from a bout of fever and dysentery from which he was suffering like one pinned to the barren train of disease – the inevitable consequence of camping beside a wretched sluggish stream, swarming with mosquitoes on the impatient fluid skin of fever. Indeed they had arrived at an inhospitable dead-end, beguiled by the ancient mirage of profit and splendour; and the servant or dog was left to fend for himself. The master struggled manfully to keep an eloquent fire going after nightfall out of fear of the voiceless wings of the vampire bat which flew with the heart of darkness. He felt so weak that it seemed a feather would knock him down and he was resigned to suffer the stroke of death in whatever form it came, but preferred the end to come in broad daylight (or such as existed in the jungle) when he could hope to catch a fleeting glimpse of friend or foe, judge or executioner. . . .

The dog had scarcely swallowed the excreta half-buried in the ground when his frame began to collapse, even as daSilva himself began to feel the first slackening and ebbing of his own delirium and fever. In daSilva's fevered brain the diseased crumb turned into a symbolic antidote even as it grew into the insidious wreck and poison the animal had eaten. It was a curious sensation he was experiencing of mysterious indebtedness to an alien creature fast crumbling before his eyes into a kind of grotesque panting bag bathed in the sub-aqueous noon atmosphere of the jungle, so that everything seemed to share a dark spectrum of shadowy lights, all leather and bone, or to roll in a winding sheet of leaves which clung to the labouring body and seemed to turn to flesh or wood or a pillow of stone.

DaSilva was drawn to assist the beast in the midst of its agony, as if the dog had become an integral failing member of himself, a misdemeanour wrought by lust or disordered senses, one of his own unpredictable limbs, the beloved sack of his stomach, covering as well as gristle, the intimate skeleton he invariably took for granted because frequently it supported or nourished him. It was an extraordinary and disagreeable idea – to assume all these possessed such terrifying autonomy – but he could not shake off the impression that when these living props defected – however unreasonable the time and season they chose – he was lost.

And yet (the thought flashed in his mind out of nowhere) was he not in danger of exaggerating the capacity of each station

85

of loss by indulging in, or submitting to, the fluttering pulse of serial instinct, death-in-life, life-in-death? Such an instinct was not confined to ordeal or defection, every dreamer knew, but to the arrival of distinctions witnessing to the negative poles of fulfilment and the open reality of being, all of which became the unique deeply felt personal stuff of the conversion of slavery into freedom, freedom into responsibility.

But – even so – how could one offset ingrowing deception in the heart of every "open" solution, one might begin to welcome as the answer to be sought in the devouring computer of the jungle? Might this open reliance not draw one into self-agreement with, instead of awareness of, the riddle of complacency in the sphinx? One's hope of conquest, self-conquest, lay then even further afield than imagined, and not in an eternal sophisticated brute or ultimatum but in confessing these animals of fate to be exercises in humility, confirming one's paradoxical impotence, which sprang from grotesque dictation to, and need of, implements of growing sensibility, capable of throwing one into the void at a moment's notice. The very absurdity of this apparently helpless position made one see how intolerable it was to succumb to the brittle wiles of servant or master one had acquired (or contracted oneself to) from birth into death. Who indeed did *one* happen to be, ruling whom and ruled by whom, relying on whom and for what? It was as if all parties were caught in a crossfire of relationships whereby they were able to visualize windows of spirit by beholding the punctures or holes in every engine of material consolation supported by the mathematic of the muse. . . . DaSilva had risen from his hammock and crawled to the stream to return with a saucepan of water which he sprinkled on his trembling companion, who snapped at him in order to moisten the crown of its mouth. The cage of teeth shut fast and then yawned helplessly again, displaying the grinning and successful mask of death.

His reaction was one of instantaneous personal relief. He

was glad it was all over. Poor agonized beast! The fever was now fast abating: the sockets of his eyes continued to burn, however, giving an exaggerated even horribly rolling sensuous apprehension of the creature lying on the ground like a ruthless and intimate organ, still digesting his (daSilva's) mortal ailment. This was an involuntary living function death would be totally incapable of achieving if one were allowed to lock oneself away in the absolute prison of oneself as in the permanent frame or capture of nebulous being. . . . DaSilva had returned to stand once again on the bank of the stream with the crude saucepan in his hand; his expression lost a certain frozen and sovereign intensity to acquire a dark submissive glow in the water like a suddenly rediscovered bulb existing in the heart of nervous filaments belonging to the jungle and uplifted head high by long reeds and legs of grass. *The disentangled cord and light of resurrection was as subjective as it was concrete or phenomenal:* it was related to the continuing ebb of his fever which was fast relinquishing the knotted image of a diseased chilling sensation in his bones so that the native flood of heat in the bush was unleashed on him as of old like a welcome furnace, restoring the equilibrium of internal temperature and external flame, and reminding him he must soon conduct the burial of the faithful carcass of his dog. . . .)

7

Stevenson had broken into the caretaker's house and placed Petra with her newborn raw-skinned infant to lie in Kaiser's bed. He found himself faint after his burning ordeal during which (just before the labour ended and the child was born) he was cold as death. The combination of shock and helplessness had robbed him of speech and in fact it had seemed to him he must have actually bitten his tongue almost in half. There was blood on his lips which may have come from within or without, he did not know. The woman was oblivious to his presence, swallowed up and swallowing him up, he felt, in an enormous kind of intimate struggle and symbolic sleep in which they were fatefully and psychologically involved, as only strangers can be when they become equally strange in relation to themselves and to every cherished misconception they held. A point of recognition and contact – alien and blinding, timeless perhaps – is established like bitter ecstasy, flesh turned inside out, incredibly formed and intrusive and incalculably brutal and alive.

Stevenson fell on his knees at the edge of the river, feeling exhausted, like someone who had crawled a long way out of far savannah and from the heart of the frame of the landscape. His discovery of the body of daSilva, clinging to the ladder of the escarpment – followed by the crude assistance he had given Petra – seemed now like a recollected feature in an impending collision of approaching vehicles, drawn out of unpredictable nature, when the still living inmates try to shrink, with such violence, into the shell of the last moment which precedes the crash that an uplifted hand or half-gaping mouth or staring eye is focused in the revolving disc of place. His head was spinning with fragments of singing emotion which were so shattering and real he plucked a ripe blade of grass from the edge of the water and chewed it to assure himself he had actually survived.

It was an infantile longing, perhaps, the feeling of green milky juice in one's mouth, the irrational desire for the secure nipple between one's lips. All at once he spat. He had crushed with his teeth a tiny unseen beetle which had been descending the blade of grass. It left a spreading staircased gritty saliva on his tongue like a coating of moss or the uncomfortable vision of indigestible shell. He wanted to spit the morsel of sensation out of him but he could not help retaining something of agonized taste and bruised impact in the crown of his mouth. It restored to his mind the vivid moment of accident or disaster, he knew, in some obscure way, he was sharing with others wherever it occurred, in the taste of earthquake or sickness or rubble, milk or slime. And not only this: a personal note he could never relinquish had been struck – organic flavour or fantastic jigsaw which deepened the search for food in the indestructible host of mankind.

Stevenson roused himself to survey the responsibilities which – in this critical moment – he had inherited, those of husbandman or steward. Kaiser's stock he discovered, was the wreck of a former supply, and the stuff in Petra's sack merely a token of the wretched ration belonging to da Silva, which had been stolen from the depot at Upper Kamaria.

Had Petra concealed the bulk of the remainder, little as it was, in some other vessel so that she would never be caught with all her eggs in one basket? The secrecy of the Amerindian in the bush was as proverbial as a fetish. Stevenson felt the magical pull on his sympathies and the mingling call of duty and desire to scrape together for her something fresh and nourishing, the fertile lovely broth of a juice culled from the head of *pacaraima* or *lukanani*. He armed himself with Kaiser's hook and line, scraps of bait made from salted meat as well as dry bloodless fish looking like lumps of chalk or dough. No saying what animated image, however stale and unprepossessing the soul of disguise, would do the necessary trick. He had once seen Kaiser catch a large *lukanani* with a scrap of paper dressed with a parrot's green feather, with which he stroked beneath the skin of the river to provide the illusion of living bait.

Stevenson wormed his way cautiously along the edge of the water toward the falls, as he had once seen Kaiser do, until he came to three bald rocks, reddish and blackish in weathering and colour from periodic submersion when the river rose, and emergence when it dropped. These were now playing prominently out of the stream from the heart of a submerged crowd and they led him, like his own shadow, into the river and upon the back of rose-coloured stone whose soft rippling head and shoulders, in the body of the current, were bowed down in the secret depth of running water.

This was one of the seasonal stations where Kaiser fished and watched, in sight of his own landing, and standing upon a fluid division within the foaming blanket cast forth from the rapids baffling and inclining passing fish to snap like angry dogs at curious iridescent reflections, diving within the field of a bubble.

Stevenson fashioned flying bait on Kaiser's hook and tossed the line upstream, letting it slide past him and whisking it out and up again each time. He would have to hurry if he were to catch anything. A cloudburst of dwindling illumination, the skylights of late afternoon, lay on the river like scales of sun upon the organ of the rapids. The air began to turn somnolent and dull, the scales of musical light began to darken and in their place grew dark humps and fins, vague presences of silver denoting trace or settlement, reverberation or obstruction.

Something he could not fathom drew his attention and the thread of his glance appeared to jerk towards the landing; a shadow had moved there, and yet it was more than this, in the present fading light and strengthening gulf of distance, something more solidly draped, and yet floating still on his mind at a certain remove from concrete reality. Whatever it was – more than reflection if less than man – it had either vanished into the door of the building or passed around a corner and into the wall of the bush. The compulsive link he felt with the apparition gave him a cruel start. Then he realized, and was consoled by the thought, that Kaiser may have returned from his visit to Bartica town. He had been so intent on the task in hand he may not have caught the drone of the outboard engine until it blended with the orchestra of the falls. The question arose – where had Kaiser moored his dinghy? Stevenson recalled the lines of rapid inspection he had made a short while ago, during which he had observed a corial fifty feet bottomside of the landing. He had wondered whose it was then but now he sensed it was clear that this was a likely place – under the cloak of the trees and hidden from the influence of the sun – for Kaiser to lodge each vessel at his disposal for fishing, hunting or driving downriver. . . .

At last he stopped and wound the line around the fishing-rod and made his reluctant way back to the bank of the river, full of disappointment that he had caught nothing. The swift blur of the tropical evening was beginning to take the edges away from everything and even the bald heads of stone he had stepped gingerly upon were like diminished flakes which had given him a glimmering footing a hair's breadth above a black voluminous grave of motion. He approached the cottaged veil of Kaiser's house which was now drained of both the convention of time and the bubble of reflection and raised to an elevation above the close river of darkness like a standing quarry of gloom, higher than the medium of light it had once involuntarily absorbed and manifested. Stevenson was stricken with the fear of another night in the jungle created out of a single undying moment, which was neither the superficial stoppage nor the ornamental vigil of time but the self-reversal of painted clarity into groping senses of mission, the sharing of the inner flood of frightful humility or unvarnished blindness in the heart of the clock. He was now stumbling about the house calling for Kaiser and Petra but no reply came out of the pages of darkness which were settling more swiftly than he had calculated. With nervous hands he lit match after match, not knowing how to read the address of scorched fingers in the blot of his eyes. At last he found a lantern and the steady flame he now lit kept at arm's length the hordes of night which pressed along with him to lean over Kaiser's bed. The league of his own enormous branching shadow – fishing for a secret, Amerindian-wise – seemed to flow and confirm that the woman had fled with the child of fortune on her back.

His reaction was one he had never bargained for: a hideous

consternation arose within the empty room and under the silent flood of the clock, anger and rebellion, the folly of helplessness within the dead-end of pride. He felt as if he had been plundered of everything he, too, had once plundered in the gamble of images of hate and love. It was a sickening confession of ordeal within and without, the resurrection of clamouring motive, a rude snapping and snarling at his own conscience like the violence of a dog which bites until it bleeds to life the dead hand of its old master. The moment had come to hold himself in leash, to make a close prisoner of himself now that the greatest and subtlest trial of himself had commenced within the fixations of pride and the processes of humility. The prosecution would tax him to the uttermost and draw from him bestial resources of fear and strength, the furies of anguish and rage at the thought of witnessing their own subjection.

Love and hate had been instructed to join painted hands, hands of arresting blood or fame, in a ferocious enigma. Was this the bond of propriety they were taught to exorcise, the treaty they had to sign, the art of expediency they must practise? Whatever ornamental refinement and hypocritical stoppage of cruelty they wished to impose – how could one dare to reproach them in the light of the basest ingratitude and heartlessness of history they wished to check, if not overcome? Unclasp them, out of altruistic pretensions, if one must – at one's peril. For they were the stable (because unself-righteous) constitution one had set over one's untrustworthy self to restrain the wildest unimaginable panic in pursuit of the ghosts of longing and fantasy. Who could say how dangerously arrogant one might become if one followed one's purest instincts of absolute rage for good? If unclasp them one must – in favour of ideal goodness and clarity of image – which hand became the free hand of hate and whose the necessary handcuff of love? Stevenson found it hard to endure the thought of such secrecy, double-dealing and incalculable obstinacy in the heart of man or woman, machine or god.

Why should someone – whom he had assisted in every way he knew – fly from him out of suspicion or fear? He had been repulsed and bitterly humiliated. Petra bore an uncanny resemblance to the muse or mistress he had defended, it seemed now, not months or ages past but within the span of one claustrophobic moment. Within such a memorable embrace she remained eternally beautiful and strong and primitive. More cunning and shocking and unpredictable than he dreamed nevertheless: she had seen through his duplication of sentiment to the core of his necessity to mount a guard over himself. . . . Stevenson sank to the edge of the bed, half-asleep on his feet and yet half-confused and trembling to run out into the bush and defend himself from shocking accusations of waste and incontinence he had never committed. . . . He was appalled at the spectre of his own dreaming mind locked in a cell of time in the forest. . . . Would one ever learn to submit gently to the invisible chain of being without attempting to break loose and run after something or someone one knew as inadequately and helplessly as one knew one's own hand upon one's own heart? Where lay the source of such passionate dread of injustice or misery?

Stevenson dreamt he arose and approached his own chained diminutive hands on the wall. He stood within the false, uneasy circle of light spread by the lantern on the floor, to unhook the clock and begin winding the spring, listening to the startled conscientious sound time made anew, like the wavering crunching of a hard dry biscuit or metallic crust.

He had not eaten since morning and the grinding teeth of time invoked within him a brutish witness, half-master, half-servant of hunger, appearing on his behalf. The involuntary beast and its universal flesh and prey were struggling to support as well as encompass him, rolled into one objective and subjective instrumental plea which he must now resist as well as appraise in another capacity as his own sole independent judge. It was a complex undertaking, judge, witness, accused, three in one. He turned from the face of the clock on the wall and crossed with the spring of his own shadow which darted away from him on the ground, towards the light of the moon that lay on the door leading into the body of the house. The late worn features of the moon had indeed risen, dispersing a tattered filthy blanket of cloud and the dust of effulgent alarm mingling with a watery stroke of mist, coming out of the dissonance of the falls, settled like an open wreath of crumbling judgment through a window on the floor of the hall.

In condemning himself and sentencing himself to accept a certain mission or vocation (wherever he happened to be) Stevenson felt the thorns of conviction: he would save not only a vital crown and spark but the true lost life of father and friend as well. Here was the royal person whose flesh of both tribe and trial he shared, the endless trial by one's self-created peers, ancient and new, drawn out of each unprejudiced moment, unprejudiced because it was now equipped in the sober heart of every confession to enact the law as well as to preserve the timeless process of discovering and distinguishing its own limitation of the law.

There was a cupboard in the hall in which he rummaged to the tune of half-a-dozen biscuits, half a loaf of green bread and a tin of sugar. He sprinkled the sugar on the biscuits (discarding the mildewed bread) and ate like one conducting a ravenous inward dialogue with a strange principle and sentiment. The crystal explosion of the sugar as he chewed was matched all at once by a sliding scratch of his feet on the floor. He narrowly averted falling and bowed his head to scrutinize, in the filtered light of the moon, what appeared to be well-ordered decimal points scaling the ground.

He had left a gap in this juridical and mathematical procession which, however, lost not an instant in repairing itself. There was a line of arrivals and a line of departures, and as he followed these he became aware of a crouching sack in a corner, half-upright, half-draped over itself. A rent had been skilfully cut in the middle into which *acoushi* ants were entering and returning to alight once more in file on the floor, each bearing its faint pearl or grain of rice.

The moon was now standing on the trees across the river and the line of insects emerging from the caretaker's house appeared – in the bright deceptive light – to loom or join the decimalization of silver reflection, lying across the current of the river, like swollen grains ceaselessly moving and undulating upon a dense shining thread. If indeed this was the premise of an orderly division of labour in nature, which blended organization and reflection into an undeviating uniform performance for Stevenson, it was no more substantial, he dreamed, than the mirroring of diversity would have been. The uniform burden of place was neither nearer nor farther from the truth of being than the diverse gambols of station.

Diversity invited one to assume dramatic veils over functional roles which, like characters in a play, however apparently varied in action or motive – sleepwalking and still vigilant – were all the serial creation of one agent or person; uniformity coincided with a monotonous unenviable rhythm, like that of the industry of ants or bees, possessing nevertheless an astronomical undwindling patience, resembling the mysterious personality of the stars, shining for one collection of men against the eclipse of their individual sun.

The open-and-closed shutter of dream, the bitten cry in the night, the language of the heartland, relying as it did upon a curious jigsaw of intangible resources, set in viable perspective, matching darkness and light, by the recurring implosion of a sound or a word, was capable of claiming the unique eye and voice of the animal in the mind, drawing one to an appreciation of constructive mission or creative meaning which lay in consuming every total act of self-evident choice of precipitate order, chaos or diversity.

Order and diversity were the obsessed ground of witnesses in oneself to a goal and centre of Unmoved Being, which one grew to confess one shared, after all, on the crumbling border-line of confirming or pronouncing a fresh judgment on oneself and in relation to one's own value. . . . This was the greatest capacity for prejudice and error one possessed accompanied by the greatest opportunity and privilege to invoke the endless subject of reason in responsibility. . . .

A cloud drew itself like a blot over the moon and the caretaker's house vanished.

The bush appeared to acquire the imitative list of a gro-tesque pendulum in the dense creation of the watch over the jungle. It was as if one had taken a drunken stride forward and upward and Kaiser's house had been abolished in the process – or if not this, a reluctant step then back into the past and the house lay still in the creative ruin of the future. Whatever the visionary step one may have involuntarily taken the phenom-enal way or achievement in view was the same: the depot had vanished into the black invented rafters of past and future like a coal sack tilted out of a thoroughfare of fires to divide the nebulous origins of water from clustering sparks of stars.

The narrow but open band of the river, uncertain as its shape and place at first had seemed, acquired the faint but resolute illumination of the Milky Way within the obscure metallic night of the forest. It oozed like a vague sponge which was able to draw into itself every sprinkle of light, seeping through the roof of smoke half-concealing the sky until one's eye grew accustomed to the partial loss of moon or stars or sun (like a creature in ageless procession of learning to see across the watershed of the dark) and one began to perceive clearly, after a while, the long extended loop of the river, turning into an endless crack in the floor or prison of the landscape.

Through the tilted broken skylight of the moon the joints of the river appeared to climb rather than actually fall and to establish an open winding traverse like an unfinished script which – in the nature of exposure and expedition – had been half-washed away into a message of timeless incompletion or realism in association with charred foundations, Kaiser's couple of coal sacks at Lower Kamaria and Upper Kamaria and Stevenson's ruined vessel of love which he confounded with his own premises, clearing and resthouse, that had also been erased by the black sponge of light. Until they seemed three glimmering stepping stones along the map of the river, stationed to bridge one's awareness of dual proportion – the current bed the living stream advertised as well as every ancient vicarious depression of the wavering life or death of light it seemed to devour or to have once devoured. The strange brooding fact of the matter was – the nebulous coal sacks against the bank of the river divided the existing channel from da Silva's giant coffin in the heartland which the river had once occupied and abandoned before taking up its present channel. The long forgotten presence of this ancient riverbed preserved a strict crack in the body of the jungle like the frailest constellation of dust or milk.

And so the longest crumbling black road Stevenson followed in the scorched or drowned footsteps of every witness, accuser and accused, judge and muse, in the fiery submersion and trial of dreams, was but an endless wary flood broken into retiring trenches or advancing columns, all moving still towards fashioning a genuine medium of conquest, capable of linking and penetrating the self-created prison-houses of subsistence, these being the confusing measure of vicarious hollow and original substance.

Stevenson did not know where the road led. He only knew it was there.

POSTSCRIPT

POSTSCRIPT

Zechariah Stevenson disappeared somewhere in the Guianan/ Venezuelan/Brazilian jungles that lie between the headwaters of the Cuyuni and Potato rivers.

In the half-burnt down shell of the small resthouse where he was last seen by a couple of pork-knockers was found a bundle of scorched papers: when pieced together they grew into fragments of letters to one Maria and three shattered poems, two *(Troy* and *Amazon)* practically destroyed and the other *(Behring Straits)* so browned by fire that some of the lines were indistinguishable.

Troy

The working muses nourish Hector
hero of time: like small roots that move
greener leaves to fathom the earth.
This is the controversial tree of time
beneath whose warring branches
the sparks of history fall. So eternity to season. . .
. . . the barbaric conflict of man.

. . . must die first to be free.
. . . .
. . . the secret
root of the heart. And musing waters dart
like arrows of memory over him, a visionary:
smarting tears of the salty earth.

The everchanging branches of the world, the green
loves and the beautiful dark veins in time
must fall to lightnings and be calm in broken
        compassion:

but the wind moves outermost and hopeful
auguries: the strange opposition of a flower on a
        branch to its dark
wooden companion. . . .

Behring Straits

The tremendous voyage between two worlds
is contained in every hollow shell, in every name
        that echoes
a nameless bell,
in tree-trunk or cave
or in a sound: in drowned Asia's bones that glisten
        in nameless
shifts: white bones that are a proud fleeting
incongruity like a Mongolian journey, a log book
        in clouds

. . . .
          . . . .
. . . .

Untangled the trees mount to the sky
and the silence is filled with a different wave like
        sound
that alters dimension. The cool cave of ship
is sudden bleached with sun,
is drowned in a fluid ecstasy that devours and is
        devoured in turn
external still profound.

. . . .

. . . .
. . . .
The voyage between two worlds
is fraught with this grandeur and this anonymity.
    Who blazes a trail
is overtaken by a labyrinth
leading to many conclusions.
        . . . .
. . . .
. . . the incomplete discovery of the world
in the blueness of its delicacy . . .
. . . must rise unerringly
into an outline or alienation or history
into a bond that both strengthens and severs in the
        movement of life:
. . . .
earth waits for the continual voyager
Who dances on mortal ground.

Amazon

. . . world-creating jungle
travels eternity to season. Not an individual artifice –
this living movement
this tide
this paradoxical stream and stillness rousing reflection.

This living jungle is too filled with voices
not to be aware of collectivity
and too swift with unseen wings
to capture certainty.

Branches against the sky tender to heaven the
        utter beauty
. . . storehouse of heaven

. . . .
The green islands of the world
and the bright leaves lift their fragile blossom of
       sunrise
. . . And the setting sun
wears a wild rose like blood. . . .

ABOUT THE AUTHOR

Wilson Harris was born in New Amsterdam in British Guiana, with a background which embraces African, European and Amerindian ancestry. He attended Queen's College between 1934-1939, thereafter studying land surveying and beginning work as a government surveyor in 1942, rising to senior surveyor in 1955. In this period Harris became intimately acquainted with the Guyanese interior and the Amerindian presence. Between 1945-1961, Harris was a regular contributor of stories, poems and essays to *Kyk-over-Al* and part of a group of Guyanese intellectuals that included Martin Carter, Sidney Singh and Ivan Van Sertima. His first publication was a chapbook of poems, *Fetish*, (1951) under the pseudonym Kona Waruk, followed by the more substantial *Eternity to Season* (1954) which announced Harris's commitment to a cross-cultural vision in the arts, linking the Homeric to the Guyanese. Harris's first published novel was *Palace of the Peacock* (1960), followed by a further 23 novels with *The Ghost of Memory* (2006) as the most recent. His novels comprise a singular, challenging and uniquely individual vision of the possibilities of spiritual and cultural transcendance out of the fixed empiricism and cultural boundedness that Harris argues has been the dominant Caribbean and Western modes of thought.

Harris has written some of the most suggestive Caribbean criticism in *Tradition the Writer and Society* (1967), *Explorations* (1981) and the *Womb of Space* (1983), commenting on his own work, the limitations of the dominant naturalistic mode of Caribbean fiction, and the work of writers he admires such as Herman Melville.

Following the breakdown of his first marriage, Harris left Guyana for the UK in 1959. He married the Scottish writer Margaret Burns and settled in Chelmsford. Thereafter, until his retirement, Wilson Harris was much in demand as visiting professor and writer in residence at many leading universities.

Jan R. Carew

Black Midas

Introduction: Kwame Dawes
ISBN: 9781845230951; pp. 272; 23 May 2009; £8.99

This is the bawdy, Eldoradean epic of the legendary 'Ocean Shark' who makes and loses fortunes as a pork-knocker in the gold and diamond fields of Guyana, discovering that there are sharks with far sharper teeth in the city. *Black Midas* was first published in 1958.

Jan R. Carew
The Wild Coast

Introduction: Jeremy Poynting
ISBN: 9781845231101; pp. 240; 23 May 2009; £8.99

First published in 1958, this is the coming-of-age story of a sickly city child, sent away to the remote Berbice village of Tarlogie. Here he must find himself, make sense of Guyana's diverse cultural inheritances and come to terms with a wild nature disturbingly red in tooth and claw.

Neville Dawes
The Last Enchantment

Introduction: Kwame Dawes
ISBN: 9781845231170; pp. 332; 27 April 2009; £9.99

This penetrating and often satirical exploration of the search for self in a world divided by colour and class is set in the context of the radical hopes of Jamaican nationalist politics in the early 1950s. First published in 1960, the novel asks many pertinent questions about the Jamaica of today.

Wilson Harris
Heartland

Introduction: David Dabydeen
ISBN: 9781845230968; pp. 104; 23 May 2009; £7.99

First published in 1964, this visionary narrative tracks one man's psychic disintegration in the aloneness of the forests of the Guyanese interior, making a powerful ecological statement about man's place in the 'invisible chain of being', in which nature is a no less active presence.

Edgar Mittelholzer
Corentyne Thunder
Introduction: Juanita Cox
ISBN: 9781845231118; pp. 242; 27 April 2009; £8.99

This pioneering work of West Indian fiction, first published in 1941, is not merely an acute portrayal of the rural Indo-Guyanese world, but a work of literary ambition that creates a symphonic relationship between its characters and the vast openness of the Corentyne coast.

Andrew Salkey
Escape to an Autumn Pavement
Introduction: Thomas Glave
ISBN: 9781845230982; pp. 220; 23 May 2009; £8.99

This brave and remarkable novel, set in London at the end of the 1950s, and published in 1960, catches its 'brown' Jamaican narrator on the cusp between black and white, between exiled Jamaican and an incipent black Londoner, and between heterosexual and homosexual desires.

Denis Williams
Other Leopards
Introduction: Victor Ramraj
ISBN: 9781845230678; pp. 216; 23 May 2009; £8.99

Lionel Froad is a Guyanese working on an archeological survey in the mythical Jokhara in the horn of Africa. There he hopes to rediscover the self he calls 'Lobo', his alter ego from 'ancestral times', which he thinks slumbers behind his cultivated mask. First published in 1963, this is one of the most important Caribbean novels of the past fifty years.

Denis Williams
The Third Temptation
Introduction: Victor Ramraj
ISBN: 9781845231163; pp. 108; 23 May 2009; £7.99

A young man is killed in a traffic accident at a Welsh seaside resort. Around this incident, Williams, drawing inspiration from the *Nouveau Roman*, creates a reality that is both rich and problematic. Whilst he brings to the novel a Caribbean eye, Williams makes an important statement about refusing any restrictive boundaries for Caribbean fiction. The novel was first published in 1968.

Roger Mais
The Hills Were Joyful Together
Introduction: tba
ISBN: 9781845231002; pp. 272; October 2009; £8.99

Unflinchingly realistic in its portrayal of the wretched lives of Kingston's urban poor, this is a novel of prophetic rage. First published in 1953, it is both a work of tragic vision and a major contribution to the evolution of an autonomous Caribbean literary aesthetic.

Edgar Mittelholzer
A Morning at the Office
Introduction: Raymond Ramcharitar
ISBN: 978184523; pp. 208; October 2009; £8.99

First published in 1950, this is one of the Caribbean's foundational novels in its bold attempt to portray a whole society in miniature. A genial satire on human follies and the pretensions of colour and class, this novel brings several ingenious touches to its mode of narration.

Edgar Mittelholzer
Shadows Move Among Them
Introduction: tba
ISBN: 9781845230913; pp. 320; December 2009; £9.99

In part a satire on the Eldoradean dream, in part an exploration of the possibilities of escape from the discontents of civilisation, Mittelholzer's 1951 novel of the Reverend Harmston's attempt to set up a utopian commune dedicated to 'Hard work, frank love and wholesome play' has some eerie 'pre-echoes' of the fate of Jonestown in 1979.

Edgar Mittelholzer
The Life and Death of Sylvia
Introduction: Juanita Cox
ISBN: 9781845231200; pp. 318; December 2009, £9.99

In 1930s' Georgetown, a young woman on her own is vulnerable prey, and when Sylvia Russell finds she cannot square her struggle for economic survival and her integrity, she hurtles towards a wilfully early death. Mittelholzer's novel of 1953 is a richly inward portrayal of a woman who finds inner salvation through the act of writing.

Elma Napier
A Flying Fish Whispered
Introduction: Evelyn O'Callaghan
ISBN: 9781845231026; pp. 248; February 2010; £8.99

With one of the most delightfully feisty women characters in Caribbean fiction and prose that sings, Elma Napier's 1938 Dominican novel is a major rediscovery, not least for its imaginative exploration of different kinds of Caribbeans, in particular the polarity between plot and plantation that Napier sees in a distinctly gendered way.

Orlando Patterson
The Children of Sisyphus
Introduction: Geoffrey Philp
ISBN: 9781845230944; pp. 288; November 2009; £9.99

This is a brutally poetic book that brings to the characters who live on Kingston's 'dungle' an intensity that invests them with tragic depth. In Patterson's existentialist novel, first published in 1964, dignity comes with a stoic awareness of the absurdity of life and the shedding of false illusions, whether of salvation or of a mythical African return.

V.S. Reid
New Day
Introduction: tba
ISBN: 9781845230906, pp. 360; November 2009, £9.99

First published in 1949, this historical novel focuses on defining moments of Jamaica's nationhood, from the Morant Bay rebellion of 1865, to the dawn of self-government in 1944. *New Day* pioneers the creation of a distinctively Jamaican literary language of narration.

Garth St. Omer
A Room on the Hill
Introduction: John Robert Lee
ISBN: 9781845230937; pp. 210; September 2009; £8.99

A friend's suicide and his profound alienation in a St Lucia still slumbering in colonial mimicry and the straitjacket of a reactionary Catholic church drive John Lestrade into a state of internal exile. First published in 1968, St. Omer's meticulously crafted novel is a pioneering exploration of the inner Caribbean man.

Austin C. Clarke, *The Survivors of the Crossing*
Austin C. Clarke, *Amongst Thistles and Thorns*
O.R. Dathorne, *The Scholar Man*
O.R. Dathorne, *Dumplings in the Soup*
Neville Dawes, *Interim*
Wilson Harris, *The Eye of the Scarecrow*
Wilson Harris, *The Sleepers of Roraima*
Wilson Harris, *Tumatumari*
Wilson Harris, *Ascent to Omai*
Wilson Harris, *The Age of the Rainmakers*
Marion Patrick Jones, *Panbeat*
Marion Patrick Jones, *Jouvert Morning*
Earl Lovelace, *Whilst Gods Are Falling*
Roger Mais, *Black Lightning*
Edgar Mittelholzer, *Children of Kaywana*
Edgar Mittelholzer, *The Harrowing of Hubertus*
Edgar Mittelholzer, *Kaywana Blood*
Edgar Mittelholzer, *My Bones and My Flute*
Edgar Mittelholzer, *A Swarthy Boy*
Orlando Patterson, *An Absence of Ruins*
V.S. Reid, *The Leopard* (North America only)
Garth St. Omer, *Shades of Grey*
Andrew Salkey, *The Late Emancipation of Jerry Stover*
and more...